The Touch of
Honey

Book One of the Honey Saga

By J. L. Brandenburg

The Touch of Honey is a work of fiction. Names, characters, places, and incidents are the production of the author's imagination or are used fictitiously. Any resemblance to actual persons, living or dead, events, or locales is entirely coincidental.

Published in the United States by J. L. Brandenburg at DBPI.
Names: Brandenburg, J.L. author
Title: The Touch of Honey: The Honey Saga, J.L. Brandenburg

FICTION/Romance, mystery, suspense, women's fiction, adult fiction

ISBN: 9780998802404

Printed in the United States on acid –free paper

First Edition

To my children, Scott, Brendan and Bekah:

Thank you for accepting the romance I had with my characters for so many evenings and weekends. And for listening to my dreams, concerns, and fears throughout the process.
But mostly thank you for allowing me the freedom to stretch my wings while reaching for a new goal in my life.

Love,   Mom

An extra special thank you to my Aunt Jane and my friend Sam for recognizing my ability to tell a story and reminding me that we are never too old to pursue dreams.

Register at   Jlbrandenburgauthor.com

To receive a free digital copy of

Joni and Adam's character development backstory

1.

The SUV had the bad luck to begin its merge onto the highway in the midst of a high-speed chase. The vehicle came onto the road just as a van being chased by three unmarked federal cars, came up on it. Intentionally swerving, the van driver sideswiped the oncoming SUV as he passed it. The impact caused the car to spin, tip over the guard rail, and roll down the embankment.

Right up until this moment, the driver of the third unmarked car had considered himself the luckiest man on earth and possibly one of God's favorite people. Anthony Adam Jefferies became enamored at a young age by the very thought of being a part of the mystic that is the CIA. Every book he read and every movie he watched pulled him further into his fantasy life. Just the name CIA conjured up images of covert missions, titillating spy plots, and espionage storylines in which he became a major character.

Jefferies believed he was singlehandedly going to save the world and it had been his sole reason for choosing spying as his career. It was the Central Intelligence Agency that recruited him straight out of college for his physical build and strength, intelligence, foreign language skills, and almost photographic memory. He practiced diligently until he mastered the craft of spying. The clandestine fundamentals of wiretapping, dead drops, safe houses, defensive driving, and the technological advantages of spying for the Feds were thrilling to him even to this day. The paramilitary training taught him how to protect himself and think simultaneously.

All his natural instincts, along with his defensive driving skills, were put to the test as he slammed on the brakes when Jefferies saw a man in the road frantically waving. The sudden reaction threw his car into a slide and caused him to rapidly maneuver the wheel to avoid striking the man in the road.

The passenger in the now sliding car slapped the dash. "What the fuck are you doing? There's nothing you can do here. Get back in the chase." Sabastian Gramm glared at the driver. His face was flushed from the excitement of the hunt and the frustration of the interruption.

The smell of fuel permeated the air and smoke was rising from the wreck on the road below. "Look there's a body in the road. We can't risk another injury. I'll work traffic and tend to the injured. You go check on the car." The words were hurled at Gramm as the men exited their own vehicle. Sebastian set out, cursing under his breath the whole way down the hill.

The woman on the ground was trying to get up. She kept moaning, "Jack, Jack," over and over. It was the most pitiful sound Jefferies had ever heard. He used to think there was nothing he didn't love about being a spy, but somehow this accident made him feel differently.

After rerouting traffic, he knelt over the woman, clasped her hand and spoke, "Hold on, I'll stay right here. We are looking for Jack." The feminine scent she was wearing wafted up to his nose, startling him to her humanness. His voice became firm as he commanded her, "Come on, look at me. I'm right here, I'm going to stay here with you."

The agent's training overrode his emotions as he assessed her condition. He put pressure on the long, deep, and jagged cut on her left cheek. Her eyes were becoming dilated and her breathing labored with each intake of air. Looking her over, he also found deep gouges and massive contusions on her arms, legs and torso, realizing she had potentially fatal head and back injuries. The agent found it frightening when she lapsed into silence. Her stillness created a sense of determination and alarm within him. He touched her arm, stroked her face, trying to get her to open her eyes. Again, he commanded the silent figure as he physically tried to get her attention, "Come on. Look at me. I'm right here. Look at me. I'm not going anywhere."

Gramm shouted as he climbed back up the embankment, "Damn, the car caught fire before I could get the others out. There were other two occupants, but both are DOA. I'd wager a bet it was her husband and a kid judging the size of the bodies. There is a wedding ring on the driver. How about her? Look, I found her purse." Gramm had been searching for some ID. "Here we go. Her name is Joan Crawford. She's from Hampton." He read the information aloud as he walked toward his partner.

Gramm stood next to Jefferies after radioing for help and reminded him of the reason they were on this road today. "You know Wiegand is going to be pissed if those guys escape. There's gonna be hell to pay for this stunt.

You fuckin just wasted two years of surveillance work. What the hell made you stop? This isn't like you."

Jefferies stilled for a moment, pondering the question. "I...well, our surveillance was wrong. Look at this. I guess I am feeling responsible for this ...what we did here today. This lady's whole life has just changed because of our actions and faulty surveillance." The agent responded cynically, but internally was rattled by the emotions surfacing.

When the rescue helicopter arrived, Tony reluctantly surrendered her to the medics. The pilot repeated several times there was no extra space for a rider, regardless of his agent status. He would have to find another way to the hospital, but they needed to evacuate the patient right now.

Jefferies shouted at Sebastian he might want to catch a ride as he jumped into their unmarked vehicle.

Sebastian just shook his head, screaming loudly at the back of his partner, what the hell was going on in his mind. The undercover operative just shrugged off Gramm's rants, closed the car door, and gunned the engine. The car leaped into action as he started off down the road.

Time and his thoughts were his enemy today it seemed. Tony's mind wandered as he rushed to the hospital, remembering how he had gotten to this place. It had been the Special Activities Division, or SAD unit, that had taken proprietorship of him at the academy. They began specializing his training after they acknowledged the effect of his playboy good looks, self-confidence, and shiteating grin effect on everyone, or so they said. It was his debonair looks and charm that would make him a valuable covert operative. Someone had said it only helped SAD's determination to recruit him when his classmates were quick to point out, "Man, don't let his big-ass smile and those pearly whites fool you. Jefferies can be a real prick if he isn't happy."

At the start of his career, the CIA utilized him on some small ops to prepare him. This allowed them to gauge his reactions and judgment in stressful situations. His trainers had all agreed, Tony Jefferies had a natural talent for being undercover and had quickly proven himself as a covert asset to his superiors. He had been proud because even undercover he lived life cheerfully and with an enthusiasm that never faltered. He remembered feeling dissatisfied because he had bigger plans for himself - he wanted and expected more. Those roles had been too small and his advancement opportunities within the agency could easily be overlooked. His supervisors reassured him these missions highlighted his natural instincts and his ability to survive. Though he was a natural, even he had some skills that needed to be fine-tuned before they could safely drop him into a big game.

The early years had been thrilling, yet slow moving. He remembered being so eager that he reminded everyone he was a spy, just in case anyone had forgotten. Over and over he had taken greater risks and pushed to be given tougher assignments. It had been with a temperamental faith that he had joined the CIA. The fact that it was his personal mission to save his country from corrupt government officials, drug cartels, and organized crime was ticked off in his mind as his reasons for becoming a spy. If he could catch a few terrorists along the way, well even better. Back then, he thought these imaginary badges of honor would contribute to his success.

His handlers admitted he proved time and again he possessed the judicial calm necessary to prevent the lack of constant support from corrupting the agent. Clandestine services were unhesitant in declaring the wisdom of finding him a role that would afford him a sense of satisfaction for the agency and for himself. They had lauded his commitment and work ethic and consulted other agents to find a network where his ambitions might be fulfilled.

A new sub-division went operational after he had spent just a few years in Clandestine Services. Even as a young agent he was aware men in charge of national security advised the White House of complications and the desired outcomes. By bringing Secret Operations online, the government now could handle anything that could not legally go on the books. A most egregious and major deviation from the norm, the CIA would be permitted to operate on American soil, but without support from the political powers. Once fully vetted, Tony Jefferies had been one of the lucky few to become a part of SO.

Membership granted him absolution of any crime committed while on the job, as long as he was not caught.

Time flew with his mind occupied with something other than apprehension. Upon arrival, he flashed his official badge at the George Washington Hospital ER desk.

A broad smile and an official line of inquiry were sourly acknowledged by a nurse who pointed to the doctor standing in the hall. After introducing himself, Dr. Chin shook hands and identified himself as the senior trauma physician for the emergency room. After glancing at the agent's badge, he shared Mrs. Crawford was suffering from head trauma, internal bleeding, and a broken back. Treatment had been delayed due to the distance of the accident site, so at this point the TBI could go either way.

Though adequately versed in many areas, Jefferies found himself staring back at the man with a puzzled expression. Dr. Chin caught the look and paused to explain. "Oh sorry, TBI. Traumatic brain injury. The bleeding in her brain might stop and the swelling could recede on its own. If not, surgery will be required to drain the fluid, but either scenario could lead to brain damage. She is headed to surgery to stop the internal abdominal bleeding. Based on the initial assessment, this means she will no longer be able to bear children. The one bit of good news-it's likely her spinal injury is a clean break and should heal with no complications. Otherwise, the rest of her wounds are relatively superficial. A few stitches here and there coupled with a bit of plastic surgery and she should be as good as new. I gotta go, they need me in the ER." He looked at his phone and turned to go.

The agent had provided the hospital with the woman's ID he'd snatched from Gramm's hand before leaving the accident scene. Now a search for relatives could begin. But for some strange reason, Jefferies could not bring himself to leave her side. His mind projected the unimaginable grief she would suffer when she learned the others in her vehicle had perished.

His cell phone blew up with calls and texts from both Gramm and Wiegand. The perp had indeed gotten away. Jefferies argued with his boss about the effectiveness off the third car in any chase. Stopping for this accident had probably kept his cover intact, meaning there was absolutely no risk of discovery now. Playing on their vanity, Jefferies reminded them how masterfully they perform their jobs. It would be relatively easy to fabricate a believable tale and Adam Carmichael was right back in business. His partner and boss were still seething when the call ended because he would not leave the hospital.

A few hours later, the doctor found him lingering in the waiting room, drinking stale vending machine coffee, and hoping for any kind of news. Dr. Chin indicated that Mrs. Crawford was out of surgery and in the recovery room.   She was coherent enough to know her name, so she might be able to answer a few questions before her pain medication took full effect.

Standing in the doorway of the woman's room, the faint smell of disinfectant, the sterile environment, and beeping machines made him pause and think of his father. He passed away after a long and courageous battle with cancer. The agent knew he was lucky to have memories of their last conversations and sense of gratitude he had a chance to say goodbye. At the end, his father was so doped up with pain medication, he could only hope his dad remembered the constant vigil at his bedside. Jefferies hoped Mrs. Crawford might feel his presence and it bring comfort to her as well.

She was writhing, crying, and pulling at the tubes in her arms.   When he clasped her hand, the thrashing lessened. "Hey, I'm here now. I'm not going to leave you.

We're looking for your family" Jefferies stroked her hand to reassure the woman.

"Where is Jack?" She mumbled as she struggled to rise from the bed.

"Is Jack your husband?" he asked, gently pushing the woman back down.

Her head bobbed no and mumbled again, "Where is my baby, Jack?"

"Oh my God." Jefferies softly sighed. Sebastian had said possibly a husband and a child. Shit, she is calling for her son. That thought tore at his heart as the woman fell silent. The agent found his feet were glued to the floor, as he stood at her bedside, inhaling her perfume, holding her hand, and thinking 'what the fuck am I doing here.'

His thoughts of the woman were interrupted by his memories of the job. Too many things went wrong today leading to this moment at this hospital.

Tony recalled it was Sebastian Gramm who brought a rising crime boss named Vincent Gamble to the attention of the SAD administration. The Gambini family had been waging all-out war with every crime family on the east coast. Trafficking in drugs, prostitution, gambling, and anything else that would turn a dollar was a part of his financial portfolio. The pace he had been eliminating his competition was alarming to any information gathering agency, because his men were fiercely loyal and mute, leaving a complete void regarding the Gambini family in the intelligence world. What had made him of greater interest to every federal agency was his sister's recent marriage to a Saudi royal.

It was while Special Operations worked to lay the foundation of his now operational legend, Adam Carmichael, that he and Gramm became partners. Gramm had touted their physical differences as an asset to the proposed arrangement. He insisted few would connect the two based purely on their physical differences and as far as he knew, Sebastian had been right.

Tony thought about his friend and partner. Sebastian was an average looking man. He stood about 5'10" in height, but compared to his own 6'4" muscular frame, he seemed quite small. Gramm's complexion was sallow and pasty from too many hours in the office and not enough time outdoors, which put him in complete opposition of the tan and healthy complexion of his partner. Jefferies was a man of action; Gramm a man of information.

Although the agency had put much time and effort into providing him with an airtight, detailed background, any infiltration of the Gambini cartel would be a very precarious job. To be of any value, it would be a long-term plant and would require him being promoted - rising through the ranks, to be credible. That statement alone made it a challenge the arrogant agent Tony Jefferies had to accept.

The agent was at the mercy of the clock hands ticking off the minutes and his wondering thoughts. Restlessness and feelings of interloping on this family's private trauma finally sent him into action mode. Dr. Chin was no longer on duty he was informed when he asked for the man by name. Instead, he was shuttled to the evening shift nurse assigned to Mrs. Crawford's case. He finally was able to ask, "Would anyone be taking over his vigil? Is anyone coming to be with her?"

The ICU nurse efficiently flipped the papers on her clipboard, then clicked a few buttons on her laptop before answering the question. Batting her long, heavily mascaraed eyelashes at him, Nurse Judy shared Mrs. Crawford's family had died in the car accident. This information had been confirmed prior to the start of her shift. Her husband, Jake Crawford, had been in the Air Force and stationed at Langley Air Force Base. The Air Force liaison faxed documentation that both sets of parents were listed deceased and neither Mr. nor Mrs. Crawford had siblings. The paperwork also listed a son, Jack Crawford, age thirteen, perished in the accident.

Dr. Laura Inglesbe became the primary care doctor when Mrs. Crawford was transferred to an ICU private room the next morning. The doctor told the agent she intended to keep Joan in a medically induced coma for three days to monitor the swelling on the brain. With this latest information, Jefferies knew he would stay at least three more days, causing his bosses further consternation.

During the three days, Agent Jefferies felt the need to take some kind of action. First, he located a number for Langley Air Force Base, where he made contact with a First Sargent Hill. Identifying himself only as a bystander, he insisted on paying for the funerals, even after learning the military would cover the expenses. Jefferies felt some relief knowing Sgt. Hill willingly accepted responsibility for the actual arrangements; purchasing the burial sites and scheduling the funerals for Jake and Jack Crawford. The Sargent also pointed out that Mr. Crawford would be buried with full military honors and that his son would be buried next to him. The final call was to a florist for eternal lanterns and wreaths to be placed on both graves.

After the medication was stopped, Joan lapsed in and out of consciousness for three more days. Jefferies was told by the nurses her consciousness was indicative of the swelling of her brain. The agent refused to leave regardless of the numerous threats issued by his superiors. He knew his actions and the faulty intelligence he gathered had caused this woman's life to change dramatically.

Tony spent most of this solitary time recalling his life with the agency and the role they played in people's lives. Ten years into his employment, the agency had created a legend with a reputation that allowed the agent to fit right in with the miscreants he was infiltrating.

Though he had been partnered with Sabastian from the very beginning, it was him calling the shots. The agency yielded to all his demands and recommendations. When they should move, where it should happen, why this was the guy to go after, how the teams should be strategically placed...you know, just how high the CIA should jump.

Sabastian was a good friend, as well as his partner. He always supported him and was an asset to the agency in his own right. He had a knack of obtaining very detailed information and the ability to transmit it at crucial times. They had managed to get a few minor players out of the game immediately. Gramm had shared with him early on that admin was thrilled with the results of this covert operation and urged him to find ways to get deeper into his cover. It took a few years and a few murders, but he had proven his worth by securing the position of confidante to Vinnie Gamble, the head of the east coast family. With that trust, his legend, Adam Carmichael, also earned the title of cleaner and hitman for the Gambini crime family. A role he was portraying the day of the accident.

The agent received the news, Mrs. Crawford was stable enough to be removed from the critical list, after seven days. This move from the intensive care wing into a private room meant she should survive, providing her will to live remained intact, per Dr. Inglesbe. The thought of her sorrow and the disciplinary actions hanging over his head was chastisement enough to get him to now leave her side. Agent Jefferies' final act of compassion was to fill her room with a large overflowing vase of flowers. Hydrangeas, lilacs, peonies, roses and baby's breath masked the smell of hospital disinfectant. There was nothing more he could do for her…or her family.

When he stepped out of that hospital for the final time, the smell of her perfume came back to his mind. Jefferies headed back into a lonely, secret, and undercover existence, wondering how she would start over. How would she face each day, when everything she had loved, has been snatched from her? It was a question he would ponder occasionally over the next few years.

After being away for almost two weeks, he chose to go directly to his office when he arrived in Newport News. His boss, Vincent Gamble, was sitting at Adam Carmichael's desk. To distract from the obvious, Vinnie held in his hands some papers; his reason for being in Adam's private office, he explained. Although they shook hands while Vinnie expressed concern and gratitude that his number one, right hand man, had recovered from the emergency appendectomy and subsequent infection, Adam believed it was nothing more than feigned distress and an excuse for rummaging through his office. But during his ramblings, Gamble inadvertently dropped a little bomb about his god-daughter.

"I had a death in the family while you were away. My god-daughter was in a car accident. It's too bad for her, both her husband and kid were killed. She is my niece's kid. After all these years, I wouldn't know her if I saw her, but I thought it was a weird coincident that you would be in the same place at the same time. She was at George

Washington hospital too."

Jefferies thought to himself, 'well, well, well. What a freakin' coincident! Joan Crawford is the goddaughter of a mob boss.'

2.

The voice is always calm and reassuring. Again, last night the dark haired, blue eyed man called out to her. This morning, she finds herself sitting with a cup of coffee, pondering the dream and what it could mean. Why do her memories mingle with some dreams? What kind of trick is her heart playing or what sort of conflict is her mind sorting out? She recalls reading that dreams are just a string of ideas, emotions, and sensations that occur in the mind involuntarily during sleep, but that seems like a silly explanation for the nightly gathering of her anxieties and memories.

Her realistic dreams are in vivid Technicolor and full of imagery and details. These are so lifelike that even the smallest particulars are easily recalled. A full range of emotions - joy, love, passion, pain, fury, or heartache, can be felt upon waking. Sometimes the sounds of music and voices in the distance, the smell of fragrant flowers, baking cookies, and cologne fill her mind with the rich details, restoring the fading memories to new.

Yet there are times when her dreams are jumbled and fractured with only bits and pieces remembered when she wakes. Vaguely she can remember the melody of music, the sound of unclear words from a familiar voice, an endearing smile, or the scent of magnolia floating around her brain. Yet the details are lost, like a picture out of focus. These dreams remind her of a bubble bath, with lots of iridescent bubbles that touch each other, creating a larger image, but none individually provide a clear picture. These dreams are soft, quick to dissipate, and leave her wanting.

Her wedding day dream comes back with just a whiff of gladiolas or sweet pea flowers. Or it might be certain strains of music, the taste of French vanilla cake with buttercream frosting, white dresses, or military uniforms that inspire the nightly visions. An overwhelming sense of happiness, warmth, love and the possibility of a happy ending resonates when she wakes, but it is a memory she avoids in the daylight hours.

The birth of her baby boy is etched in her mind as well as on her heart. The race to the hospital, the excruciating pain of delivery, and the mind-numbing fear when the newborn did not cry is a vivid and frightening dream each time it occurs. She recalls the delivery room remained quiet. There was just the sound of silence as nurses' awaited instructions. The doctor's face was serious and attentive only to the newborn. Suddenly, the baby made a gasping sound; deeply sucking in his first breath of air. The woman watched in awe as a purple baby turned pink. Then finally, the joy of all joys, the boy wailed as he was placed on her chest. The feel of her husband caressing the child they had created was blissfully remembered. Not one moment of this dream is blurry, fuzzy or unclear, yet it is drawn from memories when she was a much younger woman.

The smell of baking cookies, Old Spice cologne, songs by the group Chicago, sounds of a crying baby, a military uniform, or a man of similar build and stature as Jake, will trigger her nightmares. Her feelings of happiness are abruptly interrupted by the sounds of metal on metal, squealing rubber, screams, the sensation of flying, the smell of fire, and then incredibly intense pain, both physical and emotional follow. Vague flashes of a hospital, a graveyard, and an enormous sense of emptiness linger upon waking. It took months for her to heal physically, but mentally the process is ongoing still today.

Grief became a way of life; interrupting her finest memories and prevented the creation of any new. The riptide of anguish routinely pulled her out, away from all familiar, leaving her gasping for air, and thrashing for her sanity. But just as swiftly, a wave would roll her back to the safety of her daily routine and recollections.

Every dream and nightmare has potential triggers and with them, a specific point of reference. All but one. The most powerful, clear, and alarmingly realistic dream of the man calling to her. A striking man with dark hair and brilliant blue eyes repeating "I am here for you, keep your eyes on me, I'll stay here with you." This reoccurring dream began after the fatal accident and continues still today. Over time and after much self-interpretation, it is her conclusion God is telegraphing through her dreams there will be another chance at happiness.

3.

An Air Force grief counselor was assigned to assist a re-entry into her life. The day the counselor tried to take Mrs. Crawford back to her home ended in a hysterical outburst, complete with tears and shouts. Memories there could reopen the barely healing wounds. Hours later, the counselor packed a couple of boxes, arranged for the dog and Mrs. Crawford to stay in a hotel until a new place could be found.

The new house is located just two blocks from the Chesapeake Bay in Hampton, Virginia. It's an airy, but small, red brick ranch with bright white trimmed windows and doors. It is just over 1100 square feet with oak hardwood floors throughout. Inside, the open floor concept reveals oak cabinets in the kitchen and built in oak storage and shelves between the living and dining room. There are two average sized bedrooms on each end of the house and one small bathroom sits between them. These three rooms are off the hallway which separates the living space from the bedrooms.

The backyard is large for a home located so close to the water. A white picket fence surrounds the entire yard, allowing Bandit, a bit of independence and freedom. A 16x18 red brick patio runs along the back of the house. The 18-foot above ground pool that came with the home was listed as an added bonus in the sales brochure. This treasure of a house also has a single car garage off the backyard, in the alley.

Someone had the wisdom to decorate this new home in a relaxing cottage style. The living room is bathed in white, blue and yellows, with scaled to size white wood furniture. In front, the windows are covered by one-inch white shutters rather than curtains, giving a spacious, open feel to the rooms. The entire house has the same color scheme along with some well-placed nautical features. It is tastefully decorated and quite fitting for the location of the house.

After just a few weeks in her home, she changed the second bedroom into an office. As a bedroom, it was a constant reminder that there would be no family to use it. Over time, Joni discovered she had come to terms with the new house because it held no memories, no past, and no ghosts. It also had plenty of little "honey do" jobs which often occupied her time and for that she was grateful.

Despite the new place, initially caring for Bandit was the only reason she could muster for getting out of bed each day. The widow tried to busy herself with the mundane routines of life. Answering mail, paying bills, and grocery shopping. None of the intensive counseling had prepared her for the absolute silence, the incredible aloneness, the finality of her loss. Overwhelming grief shattered her faith with an unimaginable force and carried her into darkness. For years on end, she crashed against unidentifiable surfaces and only after years of excruciating pain was she thrown out on an unknown beach, battered, bruised, and reshaped.

The last years of living have been serious business of healing for Joni. She had cursed her God and turned from him for allowing the devastation of her life. Often, she would wake through the night, rushing through the house looking for Jake and Jack, forgetting momentarily that they never shared this house with her. Her bereavement period was prolonged as she grieved for not one, but two. In the end, she fell back to her faith, which declared her survival also held responsibility…to actually begin 'living' again.

During the intensive healing time, she spent her days lying around with Bandit nearby, but on the floor beside the bed. Bandit would sleep on the bed on the really bad days. His body filled the massive void of space and warmed the other side, reminding her of life. It was comforting for the widow to imagine he too was mourning the loss of their family…that Jake and Jack had been important to more than just one.

Even today, her canine companion remains her primary purpose for getting up each day. By default, a daily routine began to reconstruct a sibilance of a living being. A routine that included a walk, occasionally two, playtime in the yard and a dog treat each time he comes through the door. His physical presence keeps Joni focused on today, not yesterday, which is where her heart remained.

She loves a dog for being present, but also because there is nowhere else to focus the love she has to give. Bandit, well, he is a comfort... a constant reminder of their past life and the people they loved. But sometimes he can be a dreadful reminder that she won't be waking from the nightmare that has become her life. Honestly, caring for Bandit was the only thing that has kept her from joining her husband and son's company on many long nights.

Loneliness was now her infliction. Hearing her men call to her was all she could imagine for the longest time, but now their voices are fading. Someone else saying her long cherished name, Joan Crawford, became agony. Joan finally concluded that things would have to change for anything more than an existence on earth. In an effort to begin healing, she came to think of herself as Joni and introduced herself that way.

A long, dark, six years has elapsed since the accident. Joni has managed to find the strength to make two significant changes in her life, both inevitable for her continued healing progress. Four years ago, Joni had her 'revelation' that God had allowed her to survive the accident, and it was a purposeful action. This 'ah ha moment' prompted her to take on a small paper route. The regimen of the daily activity makes her feel needed and slightly alive again. The paper route is another reason for getting out of bed now. It is a reminder that this is what the 'living' do - they work.

Solitude replaced excruciating loneliness after two more years. Over time she began to feel some fresh wants and an imperative need to rejoin the living. Joni decided she felt up to the challenge of interacting with people again. It was time for a real job, one with a social component. During her daily ritual of reading the paper, she saw and responded to an ad. The public library was looking for a librarian assistant. It simply began as an idea to get outside of the walls of the house, giving her small doses of human contact.

During the interview, the panel had asked their list of standard questions. They caught her off guard when they asked why she would be the best candidate for the job. She paused only briefly, then saw their physical reaction when she answered it would be her only daily connection with people since she had lost her family in a car accident. No further questions were asked, no call back was extended. They offered the job on the spot. Probably out of sympathy, but it was a good decision which has worked well for both parties. The duties have become almost enjoyable for her and the library had been fortunate to hire a hardworking, competent, and dependable employee.

4.

Her supervisor had innocently disclosed that Joni
was viewed by her coworkers as a poor creature in an
unfortunate position of lacking family and friends. Because
of this, she often was assigned menial tasks that most of the
staff refused. On this day, it is her work at the library that
brings reality and her dream of the man calling out to her,
colliding. Thirty minutes into sorting and filing
newspapers into the archives, an edition of the New York
Times, caught her full attention. Joni caught a glance of a
small photo on the front page that piqued her curiosity. She
opened to the article in the people section. What she
recognized was her dream man. He had been photographed
with a group of party-goers at a charity event in New
Orleans. Specifically, the article was about a fundraising
bash marred by the death of one of the attendees.

Using a magnifying glass to look closer at the photo, she studied this man's image intently. His face was vivid in her mind as she recalled her dream. Systematically, she viewed his individual features. This black and white picture shows he has the same dark eyes and hair. His broad shoulder and wide smile were the same as she recalled in his nightly visits. There is no doubt, it is him. Then the revelation became apparent. He…the man from her dreams…the gift God has promised her, is real. The image that had previously been only an apparition is a real person. Finally, a there is a name to associate with this mysterious man invading her nights. There under the caption, is his name, Adam Carmichael. She plopped into a nearby chair just briefly, stunned that she finally had a name to put with this mysterious stranger.

Over her lunch break, Joni signed onto her work computer and used the library internet to google the name Adam Carmichael. It didn't take long for a few random bits of information and a few celebrity style photos to pop onto the screen. The image she had seen in the paper was also shown, but only snippets of information. There wasn't enough personal data to shed light on where he lives, who he works for or how he earns his money to be attending such glamorous charity functions. This Mr. Carmichael is a bit less of a mystery, but she can find no reason to be dreaming of him... there is nothing online revealing an obvious connection to her life.

Joni was mentally exhausted at quitting time. Thoughts of Adam Carmichael had invaded her mind all day, just like his image and voice invade her nights. Although she now knows his name, the real mystery remains - why she would be dreaming of this particular man. But at least now she knows the identity of the promise.

5.

Miami is an alluring and whimsical place to be anytime of the year, but Miami Beach in March, well it doesn't get much better. The tropical climate is certainly warmer than an early spring day in Newport News, Virginia. His undercover alias is entitled to some welldeserved R&R, so he announced he was taking a few days off and had settled on south Florida as his destination. Adam Carmichael is vacationing in Miami Beach. He had booked a luxury suite at The Palms for his days of fun in the sun. Carmichael will just need to find a babe or two, capture the attention of the paparazzi and his cover remains solid. When he gets back, Gamble will ask about the pictures and Carmichael will brag about his successful bedroom triumphs.

The mafia hitman checked himself in the mirror and chuckled inwardly as he dressed for this impromptu meeting. Laughably, he was content with what he saw in the reflection. As the man looking back at him, decked out in fine clothing, the operative decided the chore of being Adam Carmichael has some exceptional perks. The unlimited power which brought along access to the rich and influential, freedom to choose, wine, women, money, vacations, and guns, all for the partaking. The face looking back at him breaks into a full grin because that man chooses to partake in all the perks this life has to offer. For now, Adam Carmichael was very pleased with his current lot in life.

But the agent staring at the same image frowns. That man is having trouble separating the lies, the women, and the assassinations committed by a man working for the CIA. His disillusionment with the role had been gradual. Only a few real changes had occurred for his considerable investment. He was still an agent of the CIA...what could be more glamorous or even noble? This was an acceptable line of thinking as long as Jefferies' conscious didn't rise up too often or too loudly. It had been difficult to reconcile the agency's motives were often in direct opposition with his legend's investigations, resulting in more deaths than the agent ever deemed necessary.

After the 'incident', the agent had embraced the role of Adam Carmichael and waded deep into his undercover life. The operative lost sight of his moral compass years ago and eventually morphed into the person he has portrayed for so many years. The agent was still performing his job, but the criteria for agency intervention had risen many times over the years. Now only those that interfere with the hitman's desires registered scrutiny, unless orders come from the top.

At this point in this ongoing operation, any meeting was a risk. Actual contact with an undercover operative was not a decision the agency made lightly. Getting summoned for an unplanned meeting means something disastrous has or is going to happen in his world. There was just too much at stake to risk pulling him away unscheduled. At this time, he only knew his boss, Brett Wiegand, and his handler, Sebastian Gramm, would be present. As the limo transported him to the Double Tree Hotel in Miami proper, Jefferies mentally ticked off all the events of the last several weeks as the reason for the 'get together.' When the limo pulled up to the curb, there was still nothing that gave him pause. He would just have to wait and hear it from the guys who called the meeting.

The agent knocked, then entered without an invitation. There was still no greeting from either of the men standing in the room. Wiegand picked up from the table, several computer-generated sheets of white paper and a few colored agency forms. To make sure they all understood these papers are the 'why' for this meeting, he began waving them air, specifically in the operative's face as he entered the room.

Brett opens the conversation by bellowing, "do you know what the fuck these are?"

It's obvious the reams of paper in his hand had angered him enough to demand Jefferies' physical presence. But rather than answer, he shook his head no to Wiegand's question.

"I fucking told you so. I told you that goddamn bout of consciousness years ago was going to cost you…no, us as an agency. Now look at this! Your cover is once again jeopardized. Just like I told you it would be." He concluded as he shoved the papers at Tony for emphasis.

"Well hot damn Brett, I'm happy I made your day and proved you right for a change. Yeah for me. I gave you something to gloat about, but I still have no idea what you are talking about." Jefferies grinned without taking the paper from the outstretched hand.

"Lucky for you, the NSA picked up your alias in an internet search. Someone in the loop recognized it as an ongoing covert operational mission. After NSA pinned down the location and name, they provided SO with a detailed report. That woman from the car accident is looking for you. She has been googling your name. So here we are again." The messenger threw an anxious glance at the confounded face of agent Jefferies.

Secretly Tony was alarmed as he snatched the papers from the hand of his boss. His mighty shape was stricken with fear, though outwardly it did not show. The operative had a sudden realization that outside of this room, his true identity was virtually unknown to the rest of the world. It was indeed a fortunate circumstance this information had been captured and shared.

He recalls his involvement in the accident had occurred simultaneously with a bout of consciousness resulting in a week-long vigil at a hospital and a substantial payment for two funerals to ease his guilt. He had become borderline psychotic while overseeing her medical care. For a brief time standing over that hospital bed, he had contemplated leaving the agency.

Yet once he stepped back into the role of Adam Carmichael, he appreciated his decision to follow the prevailing wisdom of his supervisors. The agent acknowledged their astute assessment on how he had almost sabotaged his career and jeopardized a major undercover operation.

Jefferies reassured the CIA that Adam Carmichael, mafia hitman, was back with gusto. From that day forward, the agent adopted the legend's scripted way of life. The returning agent knew he had been acting dangerously flaky for a couple of weeks and he resolved to mend his errant ways.   Carmichael put himself at the beck and call of

Vinnie Gamble. The life of the playboy began to fit the

operative like the tailored suits he wore. Initially, it

disturbed him, because he had not expected to enjoy

anything about being back undercover.

Jefferies remained enchanted with his lifestyle until

one day a couple of years later, he practically collided with

a woman wearing the scent he remembered from Mrs.

Crawford's room. Memories of the injured woman

pounced into his thoughts and for a few hours, doubts about

his chosen career rose once again. The "what if's" of a

normal life clouded his mind while he stood inhaling the

scent. It only took a couple of bottles of champagne, a

beautiful woman and a night of meaningless sex to get him

back on track.

Once again, the injured woman's image filled his

mind as he rapidly scanned the pages and studied the

damaging assessment report. What he found was one

documented search for his alias, Carmichael. Hardly what he would call googling. Plus, the agent was confident the CIA had complete control of his online profile. So, except for a few well-placed articles and several pictures in the name of Adam Carmichael, she would find nothing revealing or truly informative. Certainly, nothing linking him, the CIA agent, to his hitman alias.

There was a physical change in the agent's demeanor as he relaxed. "Ok, fine Brett. The woman googled me, once. What's the big deal? She's only going to find whatever the agency allows to become public about Adam Carmichael. Which isn't much? I don't see the problem. One search is nothing to worry about." Jefferies ceased to listen as the smell of her perfume returned and her agonizing sorrow flooded his mind. Oh, he was pondering the "why" of the situation briefly. Why would Vinnie's god-daughter be looking for him after all this time?

His quick physical, as well as mental recovery, went unnoticed by Wiegand. "Are you fucking kidding me? This isn't just anyone looking for you Tony. You just don't want to see the implications, once AGAIN I might add. So, let me refresh your memory. If she has remembered you, even as Carmichael, it puts you at that hospital, the same time a CIA agent was hovering over her. You identified yourself as Agent Jefferies. Don't you think Gamble has the kind of resources to bring him that information if any hint of the coincidence is found? You thought he doubted your story when you returned, remember? Do you even recall you are a part of the SO team? This is a covert operation taking place on American soil. Everything about this mission is highly illegal. If you are somehow outed, you will be disavowed or labeled a rogue agent. There is no saving you from the consequences." Wiegand shook his head as he scolded the agent.

"Ok, fine, I get your point. It seems like a needle in the haystack kind of search, but since you are worried, what do you want me to do? Go and meet her in person? Just come right out and ask her why she is looking for me?" Jefferies countered, still fingering the pages.

"Yup, that is exactly what I want. You must be a mind reader when you want to be Jefferies. Seriously, Tony, we gotta find out what she knows. It would be better if she tells you her story personally. Because if she remembers you, your time at the accident scene or hospital, well, then we will have to shut her up immediately. She will have to be relocated by Wit Sec and THAT WILL be your fault. You were worried about the damn wreck and her life. Well now, you need to worry if you are going to force her to start over yet AGAIN." Wiegand chided.

"Fine. I'll go see the lady and check out her story.

I'll bet there will be nothing conspicuous to tell you. One internet search is nothing to be alarmed about in my eyes. But what the hell, I'll check it out if it will make you happy."

Secretly, he looked forward to seeing her again. He found he was curious about what had triggered a sudden desire to look for him after all this time. At the same time, his guilt surrounding the accident made him wonder how she had survived her devastating loss. If nothing else, this little jaunt down memory lane would provide a few clear-cut answers about how people, well, this woman, survived the loss of her family.

6.

It's been five weeks since Brett summoned him to Miami to tell him about the NSA report. Adam's initial information proved the woman was not attempting to hide. Not the search for the man named Carmichael and certainly not anything about herself. A cursory investigation revealed Mrs. Crawford still lived in the city of Hampton, in fact, just a few miles from his own home in Newport News.

The agent was surprised to learn Joan Crawford was employed at the main public library building, the location of the infamous google search. It had taken little effort to get her schedule and home address. A couple of smiles and a bit of small talk and he left the building with a copy the staff schedule for the next two weeks. The informative young lady at the checkout counter flirted shamelessly, making sure the man knew she was interested as she handed over the confidential information.

Jefferies had returned the favor and googled Ms. Crawford's name when he started the investigation. There was a J. Crawford listed in the white pages. The address agreed with the slip of paper provided by the NSA. The agent then navigated his vehicle to the street to find it indeed was her home. Now he had all the personal information he needed to progress; her address, phone number and her upcoming work schedule at the library. Jefferies chuckled to himself because he had been actively working on this case for less than three days.

He staked out her house and neighborhood for two additional days, wanting to know her leisure schedule and if anyone shared her home. He noted her small but pristine house was located in a typical middle- class neighborhood. Yet it was a block from the most luxurious homes in

Hampton, all overlooking the Chesapeake Bay. It was easy to see that she was living alone, well, with a dog. It appears other than walking the dog and going to work, she is a homebody he documented in the agency report.

Today as part of his recon, he was back at the library knowing she was on duty. He could see she was at the information desk right in the center of the space, as he entered the building. Adam began his methodical walk through, ready to get his questions answered, and implement his plan to meet her.

For Joni, it had been ten weeks since she googled Adam Carmichael's name. When she looked up, she was startled to see the man from the photo and from her dreams, wandering around her library. As she stared in disbelief, she found herself comparing the picture to the man. It had not done him justice. He was much more handsome than in the photo or even her dream portrayed him. For a woman who had not experienced feminine longings for many years, she was shocked by the way her internal radar was tracking this particular man.

She had been assigned to the information desk which was her least favorite station to work. Originally, she was frustrated with her duty, but now thankful her vantage point allowed her a 360-degree view of the first floor. Visually she followed him as he aimlessly wandered through the aisles, then eventually to the computerized card catalog. She secretly glanced around now and then, watching him until he strolled right up to the counter and stood directly in front of her.

Joni's heart began to pound as he approached her. Mr. Carmichael was ruggedly and manly built by any woman's standards. His arms were noticeably muscled and his tanned body was broad at the shoulders. This man stood about 6 feet 4 inches tall. He had an easy self-assurance of power and was dressed in a perfectly tailored navy blue pinstriped suit which created an aura of a man appearing to prize his wealth and all the refinements that go with it.

When he smiled at her, his dimples reached all the way to his twinkling baby blue eyes. A mustache and goatee of more pepper than salt, framed his chiseled face. Adam Carmichael's black hair was styled well and appeared to be lustrously soft. Suddenly, she found herself wanting to run her fingers through his locks to discern this fact for herself. The smell of his cologne caused her already churning stomach, to fill with butterflies. She was feeling like a giddy teenager. Joni said a quick prayer that words would not fail her as he waited for her to acknowledge him.

As she was reverently staring at him, he was content lounging in the shy appraisal of her sapphire blue eyes, while making his own assessment. Her smiles were reluctant, but warm and inviting when they escaped. A true smile fully engulfed her face causing crinkles to form around her eyes. Adam noticed the faint scar on her cheek and remembered touching her there. This striking woman was about 5 feet 8 inches tall, trim, but with curves in all the right places. The curves of a woman who has had a baby, he recalled. Mrs. Crawford's auburn hair had begun to gray at the temple, but she was attractive still.

The god-like man gazed at her for a moment, before asking about a particular book. It took a few seconds for her to process his words because she was intoxicated by the essence of him. She shook her head to clear her mind, then said she was unfamiliar with the title. The librarian assistant then asked him about the author. It had been a recommendation, so he had no name. Together they decided to try the computerized card catalog again. After several keyword searches, Joni and Adam concluded his book would not be found without more specific information.

Walking back to the reference counter, they bumped into each other. The jolt was so hard, the man had to grasp her arm to help keep her upright. But the collision was intentional. Agent Jefferies now looked at the left hand he held clasped in his own and commented on the lack of a wedding band. In a timid way, he inquired if there was a 'Mr. Librarian.' Agency protocol; ask questions you know the answers to first. Get a good read on your target.

The way he asked, all nervous and hesitant, made her blush, then giggle. Her chuckling sound made him smile. She had an endearing warm, ear to ear, smile as she looked up from the floor. He formally introduced himself as Adam Carmichael as he extended his right hand. Then he insisted they get together for coffee later. His way of showing appreciation for her hard, yet unproductive search.

She offered her hand, introducing herself as Joan Crawford, but offered Joni as her preferred name. Then she surprised herself by quickly accepting his invitation to coffee. She realized this might be the only chance to interrogate him. The one and only opportunity to seek a lead. Any type of connection between this guy named Adam Carmichael and her reoccurring dream. This was her chance to reconcile the promise God had made to a real live person.

When Agent Jefferies exited the library, his reconnaissance mission continued. From the security of his car parked across the street, using a pair of binoculars, he scrutinized her through the large ceiling to floor glass windows on the front of the building. This surveillance was to document her behavior. He watched for her to make a phone call, log onto the computer, or attempt to make contact with anyone outside of the library. His report would record any suspicious activity, but there was nothing to write, except about her normalcy.

It was only 3 pm when they confirmed the coffee date. She mentally said his name over and over, Adam, Adam Carmichael. She kept repeating in her mind creating a sense of excitement and wonder. Finding answers to her many questions was in the forefront of her mind as she returned to her duties distracted by the event.

As the day wore on, Joni became preoccupied with self-doubt. It had not occurred to her that they were worlds apart in circumstance when she had agreed to the coffee date. She had not been afraid to want her dream to come true and believed devoutly it would become a reality. Yet now there was an undercurrent of paranoia. Still, there was a deep curiosity and a very definite longing to know more about him. Joni nursed a bit of hope that she might excite him with her dream, but then imagined the pity she would receive if she asked the bizarre questions about him invading her nights.

A nagging image of this refined man sitting with unsophisticated her flooded her mind. Throughout the day she imagined asking her questions and sharing her thoughts with him. What would he say of her if she admitted she had allowed herself to take a leap of faith in her thinking?

Believing the dream of "him" means a future of happiness with her. Her self-assurance that God would send a gorgeous, well-bred man for her to love fled her in her time of doubt. How had she kidded herself into believing something so irrational for so long? Joni had fretted over the coffee date until her nerves were taunt. She had a headache and a case of dread had taken over any rational thinking. She now shied at the very thought of being so close to his maleness.

Seven o'clock and closing time was announced by the chiming of the grandfather clock in the front lobby. Tonight, she was the last person working, making it her responsibility to secure and lock all the doors. The last straggling patron was checked out and the final cart of books shelved. Finally, at seven twenty, there was nothing left to delay her from meeting him. It was complete lack of confidence that descended over her until she finally resolved to ditch the coffee shop meet. When she exited the back door, her plan was to evade his company by rushing to her car and make her get away.

For Agent Jefferies, it had been an interesting day of surveillance. First in person and then remotely from his car. He dawdled over a cold cup of coffee as he reviewed his day to ensure his report for Gramm was factual and accurate. Mrs. Crawford was physically almost exactly as he recalled her from years past. She was prettier than he remembered, but in his memories, she still had injuries sustained from her car accident. Her height was a bit of a surprise, as was her disarming smile. Both had gone unnoticed as he agonized over his role in the accident that landed her in the hospital bed. After leaving the building, he realized her duties at the library suited her. She was quick with a smile or to offer assistance to all that asked. Occasionally she approached a wandering patron and it appeared she guided them to the area they sought.

After he reviewed his mental thoughts, he realized he was very intrigued with the woman. Reviewing the document on his cellphone, the minimal written observations described her as excellent at her job, friendly with people, and seemingly uninterested in Adam Carmichael. No phone calls or suspicious electronic activity after their meeting to report. So far, true to his initial belief, there was nothing alarming to raise suspicion.

When he looked up, he realized it was a good thing he hadn't called off the recon early, because he would have missed the signs. Her now grim expression and deliberate delay tactics could be predicted by any experienced field agent as a change of mind. The agent knew she was planning to avoid him. Curious and now suspicious, as to why the change of heart, he swiftly exited his vehicle and trotted across the street. He caught her as she locked the back door. Though she had a surprised look at when she found him standing at the foot of the steps, she graciously allowed him to take her hand. Adam explained there were two coffee shops nearby and he was afraid she might miss him since he had not specified which one. Escorting her was a simple solution to a minor problem he assured her.

Across the busy thoroughfare, the couple found the quaint coffee shop busy for this time of the day. Joni shared she rarely drank coffee away from her home because most places serve it too strong for her liking. He chuckled when she ordered her coffee hot, light and sweet. She informed him any coffee could be made tasty when it was doctored with her two favorite condiments, sugar and cream.

They had to wait briefly for a table to be cleared. Once they were seated, Joni carefully examined the spots on the Formica table, blushing at the thought of being so close to this man. She was grateful for his attention and recognized his effort to engage her in conversation. It was easy to appreciate he was a master at putting others at ease.

He painstakingly asked many questions about Joni Crawford, which led into an easy discussion about work and books. She visibly relaxed when he expressed genuine interest in her dog.

When asked how she spent her leisure time, her quick response was "Oh, I have a dog at home. Bandit is an English setter. It's funny how everyone thinks he's a long-haired Dalmatian. He has stunning brown eyes and the most beautiful face." Joni smiled and looked up at her companion when she spoke about her beloved dog. "I will take him for a walk when I get home. Then because it's late, I'll grab a bite to eat, then go to bed." She used hands gesture while talking and unwittingly divulged the importance of the dog.

The topics flowed from one to the next, gradually landing on vacation travel. Joni reluctantly admitted it had been many years since she had vacationed. For some reason Agent Jefferies, couldn't let the subject go so easily.

He insisted there must be a vacation that had become her favorite place.

Joni Crawford's head dropped forward, her gaze focused on the tabletop once again when she reluctantly shared. "Well, I went to Disney World a few years ago. When I got there and saw the crowds, I thought to myself 'what have I done.' But Mickey Mouse and his staff made the visit memorable. The staff asked every day how they could help me have a magical day. On the last day, I was the one that didn't want to come home. Since then, I tell everyone they should visit Mickey." It seemed her eyes were moist when she gazed back at him.

Adam was remorseful that he had reminded her of her sadness, but he filed away the information that it must have been a family trip at least six years ago. He also wondered if it would lead to more information about her family, but nothing more was shared.

Knowing he needed to lift the mood, he teased, "When you tell me about books, you speak with such passion and knowledge. I might try reading again. You have given me pause to rethink my position on making some time for books. But honestly, I think I might start with a naughty one. So, it will hold my interest longer."

Her cheeks flushed and she was looking down at the table yet again. "Oh, my. I think God might strike you for that comment, especially within earshot of a nun!" Joni pointed at the table behind them. "She might, and maybe should, come over and whack your palm with a ruler." She warned him with a bit of a shy smile on her lips.

His face lit up. "Oh my gosh! Are you Catholic? I mean I thought only Catholic girls worry about a nun smacking her knuckles for reading naughty books." he chided her. He found himself enjoying watching her blush and looking up at him from under her eyelashes.

"No, not practicing anymore, but the teachings stick with you for life. Or at least they have for me. I still feel twinges of guilt while looking at sexy lingerie or a half-naked man in a magazine." She confessed still blushing. Joni was surprised when she caught herself laughing with him while sharing such details about her life. She couldn't remember the last time she felt so, well, normal.

Watching the clerk preparing to lock the outside door, Joni glanced at her watch. "Oh, my look at the time. I really have to go." Joni sighed. "Thank you, Adam for the lovely evening." She slid across the booth and rose to leave, pulling money from her wallet to pay her share of the bill.

Carmichael waved her hand away. "Please put your money away. I invited you, so this is my treat. But why do you have to go, if it is not too presumptuous of me to ask?" He insisted and then questioned as she was leaving the table. He was in a state of shock. His charm had failed him. She was the first woman to want to leave his company.

Joni had made it a few feet from the table, but turned back to look at him when she answered. "Oh, I have a morning job too. I have a paper route. Thank you again for the coffee." Her mind was racing and her thoughts were filled with a strange new zest for life. Joni Crawford wondered if she would ever be the same again after this magical evening.

Adam quickly exited the booth before she made a complete getaway. He pulled out his wallet, flipped through some bills, and dropped money on the table, not waiting for the check. He pushed open the door, waiting for her to pass in front of him, then asked about her plans for the next day. It had been such a pleasant evening, could he please see her again tomorrow?

Joni felt her heart start fluttering again and her feet momentarily paused. She not only survived but had actually enjoyed this evening. "Sorry Adam. But I would take a rain check for another time." she offered, wondering what had become of her brain when it extended the future invitation. "I need to till my garden and gets some plants in the ground. I'm already a couple of weeks behind schedule."

She just kept feeding him information. Agent Jefferies quickly fired off several inquisitive questions about gardening. What did she like to grow? What was her favorite vegetable? What is and why did she use only heirloom seeds?

"It sounds like a very serious undertaking and yet interesting. Joni, I want to see you again. I am offering my services to you. May I please join you tomorrow, to help with the garden?" Adam was almost begging her. Of course, he was hoping to do more intelligence gathering, but desire to spend time with her was also part of his motivation.

Joni was thoroughly intrigued by this man trying so hard to show interest in a topic he certainly was only using as conversation. She felt sure he'd never seen the end of a hoe or worked with a piece of equipment like a tiller. Not the way he is immaculately dressed she thought. Against her better judgment, she acquiesced, but she also suggested he call when he was up and ready to come over. He appeared happy about the counter offer and immediately placed both her home and cell phone numbers in his cell as she disclosed the numbers to him.

Throughout the conversation, they had been walking and were now standing at her car. He took a small step forward, invading her personal space as he lightly kissed her on the cheek.

"I can't wait to see you again. Until tomorrow." He whispered to her

Joni was shocked when out of her mouth fell out the words, "me too." Her fingers caressed the spot on her cheek during her drive home. She blushed furiously then laughed at herself when she realized she was grinning like the Cheshire cat. All from a stranger's touch.

7.

When she arrived home, sleep was elusive as the events of the evening with Adam Carmichael replayed in her mind. At times, the giddy feelings from his smile and his touch gave her hope and the thought of possibilities. But in the next second, a sense of guilt and Jake's memory would rise from her past and take a swipe at the giddiness.

Exhaustion finally overtook her reflection of the night. She slept soundly until the sound of Bandit's growling alerted her. Joni was now wide awake, fully alert, and straining to hear any type of unfamiliar noise. Bandit would not calm, regardless of her constant quiet shushes and reassurances.

Cautiously and silently, she rose from the bed. She decided to take a 'better safe than sorry' approach and retrieved her 12-gauge shotgun from behind the bedroom door. Joni was raising the gun to her shoulder as she turned the corner into the living room. Bandit was on the couch, at the window, and growling. A silhouette of a person near the porch swing could be seen when she peeked out the shutters.

Her body went rigid as she pulled herself erect and crept to the door. Quickly she flung open the interior door and then threw the storm door open, hoping for the element of surprise. Turning right, aiming the weapon at the silhouette, Joni pumped a round into the chamber, hoping the sound of a shell being readied would terrify the person at the other end of her gun.

As the sound of the shell being loaded into the chamber filled the air, she heard Adam saying, "I surrender. Sorry, I think I woke you." He began to raise his hand above his head while smiling with a very wicked twinkle in his eyes. "I didn't mean to scare you. When I said I wanted to spend the day with you, I meant the entire day.

Little did I know it would begin at 4 am, but if this is what you do, then I'm here to help. You are right, I should have warned you I was coming, but I didn't want to wake you any earlier than necessary. I am sorry I frightened you." He advised as the gun was lowered slightly.

Joni was captivated by the sight of him, but narrowed her eyes. With complete authority she demanded, "How did you find my house? I know I DID NOT give you my address. I only gave you my phone numbers."

"That's easy. I followed you home," he smirked, quite proud of himself, his hands still slightly raised above his head.

Throwing her most hateful scowl at him, she hoped he would realize this was not a funny situation. His presence on her porch had frightened her and he needed to know it.

The compelling expression on her face spoke to him because his grin faded. He quickly explained, "Wow, I'm just kidding about following you Joni. I checked White pages online. The number you gave me synced up with this address. So, I took a bit of a gamble when I couldn't get you off my mind. Look at me. See, I went home and changed my clothes."

That explanation made perfect sense, about how he had found her address. Him wanting to be here so soon, well that was something else altogether. Despite the caution she naturally exhibited, something about him compelled friendly confidence and she found herself relaxing in his presence.

Joni caught a glimpse of herself in the window, standing on the porch in her lightweight cotton nightgown, with a shotgun. She was holding at bay a very attractive man insisting he wanted to spend quality time, hell any kind of time, with her. It was a bit of astonishing news to her.

Adam noticed the sudden flush in her cheeks. "Shall we go inside so you can get ready for the day? I assume you don't carry this with you all the time," he suggested as he reached out for the shotgun.

Joni ignored his outstretched hand, she pulled the barrel from his reach. She had no intention of relinquishing her weapon to him but instead backed up, opened the door, and waved the shotgun as an unspoken invitation for him to join her inside. She gave a low laugh and with unruffled sincerity chided, "Nope, I use a 9MM to accessorize my daytime attire."

Not certain if she was serious, he decided this is a woman of action and determination. One he would need to watch closer than he had initially planned. Adam

Carmichael immediately stopped in his tracks as he stepped in the house. "What is his name again?" he asked when he encountered the dog.

Bandit blocked his entry into the house, but he was no longer growling. He sniffed the back of Adam's fisted hand when it was cautiously offered. Joni imagined Adam's ability to put others at ease, must apply to dogs too, because they became friends instantly. Soon Joni heard him calling Bandit "the big dog". Joni interpreted Bandit's immediate acceptance as a good sign but was still secretly pleased when he shadowed her into the bedroom as she departed to make herself more presentable.

She rejoined Adam after changing into a pair of bib overall shorts and a T-shirt. She was taken aback to find Mr. Carmichael standing in her kitchen, looking suspect, but of what, she was unclear. Looking around for coffee he offered before she asked the question. Joni pulled the can of coffee from the upper cabinet as he began filling the coffee carafe with water. Already it seemed like they were working as a team. Joni shook her head and smiled to herself at the image that leaped into her brain.

They poured mugs of coffee when the sputtering of the machine told them the brewing process was complete. He wanted his black then laughed while he watched Joni stir four tablespoons of sugar and lots of cream into her cup. She reminded him she still liked it light and sweet, even at home.

As they talked, Adam subtly continued his visual surveillance of the interior of her home. The place was furnished luxuriously simple, but a telling truth became evident as he studied the rooms. It lacked personal items like photographs and knick-knacks; the things that make a house a home. The place where he did notice some homey touches was the kitchen. He made a mental note he might use her love of cooking to his advantage in the future.

The newspapers arrived on the doorstep with a thud. Adam carried the bundles of papers from the porch to the car, then folded himself into the backseat on the passenger side of her Escape. Their plan would mimic her typical routine. She would fold and rubber band the papers then toss a few in the back seat. Adam would take one side of the street and she would take the other.

Her days had been one just like the other for many years. Each one beginning quiet and sedate. But today he insisted on music – loud, rowdy country music. He sang with the radio and encouraged her to "sing along with Adam" when he found the Christmas sing-a-long with Mitch Miller CD in the console. Adam attempted to palpitate some life in the day by prancing and dancing up to the porches.

Laughter erupted from her easily on this morning. She felt admiration for his zest for life and could contemplate the unattainable on this day. Joni was thinking how happy she felt and how unusual it was to smile. "I would like to treat you to breakfast as a thank you for all your hard work and the floor show. Have you ever eaten at Tommy's?"

He felt success that she participated and smiled. Adam shook his head no in response to her question as he rubbed his hand across his t-shirt, showing off his six pack abs and replied, "Breakfast sounds delicious. I am surprised how hungry I am at this hour, well, because I rarely am up this early."

He began his mental profile based on what he had learned thus far. During the car ride delivering the papers, she had revealed glimpses of insight into her personality and life. Joni was likely an introvert and worried about being an inconvenience to others. Adam deduced this just from the way she listened to music in her car, but then he had started with an unfair advantage, knowing about her tragedy. She was timid. Too afraid to do anything that might draw attention to herself, like turn the radio up loud, sing at the top of her lungs, or dance to the music. Today he got her to laugh, out loud and often, during the short time they were in the car.

At Tommy's, they shared a few childhood stories, personal work achievements, art and literature preferences, but mostly they each came to the realization they were comfortable with each other. After eating the breakfast and lingering over several cups of coffee, neither was ready for the magical spell to be broken.

It was only 6:30 am when they left the restaurant and arrived back at her house. "What should we do now?"

"Actually, it is too early to fire up the tiller. It makes too much noise. I do not want to make enemies of my neighbors. Especially the ones that sleep in on Saturdays. Honestly, if it were just me, I'd go back to bed for a couple of hours."

"That's a great idea. I could really use a couple of hours of shut-eye myself. You know, since you were on my mind, I didn't sleep much last night. Where should I stretch out?"

"You want to stay here?" She was thoroughly shocked by his request.

Adam glimpsed at the living room and realized it held an apartment length couch. Certainly not a place for him. 'Is there any way she is going to let me into her bed, already,' Adam thought wistfully? The man just grinned and nodded as he slyly looked at the sofa and then glanced toward her bedroom.

She hesitated briefly but was secretly admiring his boldness. "Well, I guess you can join me in here. You are certainly not going to fit on the sofa and I know from experience the chairs are not comfortable." She stepped into her bedroom and opened the closet door. "OK. Here you go. You take the right side. But you need to know up front Mr. Carmichael, I'm not that kind of girl," Joni giggled as she handed him a blanket.

"Well, exactly what kind of girl would you happen to be?" He was looking at the bed with a puzzled expression on his face. "Hey, why did you make your bed this morning? Afraid I might see your funny sheets?"

Joni's face remained serious as she reluctantly replied, "Ha, ha. No. I just don't sleep under the quilt and sheets. I use a blanket and sleep on top. See, this is my blanket," She pointed at the heap of fabric laying at the foot of the bed.

He smirked as he said, "That seems a bit odd for someone who says she is anally organized and set in her ways. Do I dare ask why?" It was the agent at work with this question.

She strained over the very personal and painful question, yet believed he was justified in expecting a truthful answer from her. "Well, frankly, I believe a turned down bed is a place to be shared and enjoyed with someone you love. I guess…well, it's hard to lay in this bed alone. You see, I was married before, but my husband and son were killed in a car accident. I'm sorry, but that is all I want to say about it. This is a place for me to sleep, but it is not a place of comfort or pleasure for me anymore," she croaked and waved her hand in front of her face. The tears welled up in her eyes when she looked up and before she could turn away from his stare. Quickly Joni laid on the bed then rolled to her side. She closed her eyes with hope of sleep rather than tears.

The agent settled onto his side of the mattress, astounded she would agree to share her bed with him. But with her agreement came two valuable bits of information about how Mrs. Crawford had survived. He found himself detecting an unmistakable need for human companionship

and kindness in her life. Secondly, she enlightened him that

she is very much still wounded. That she slept ON a bed,

but not IN it. Sleep was her only reason for being in bed.

8.

At first, he found the silence between them oppressive, but he was able to doze off for a brief time. The fact that he hadn't slept for several hours should have resulted in a deep slumber, but the fact that she was right there, lying next him, kept running through his mind. All the times thoughts of her crept in his mind and the unlikely miracle that has caused them to cross paths again had a disturbing effect on his investigation.

The small, silver triple photo frame on her nightstand captured his attention. He sat up and examined the pictures closely. In the first frame must be a photo of Jake in his uniform. Her husband appeared to have been an average man. Not handsome or plain, not small or large, not broad or narrow, but extremely blonde. He had a broad, high cheek boned face with a tanned complexion. It was easy to see his admiration of the photographer in his twinkling eyes.

In the middle frame was the same man in casual attire. Standing next to him was a boy of about ten. Jack shared the same blonde hair as his father, but had inherited his mother's nose and warm, dimpled smile. He was a cute kid and a good blend of both his parents the agent thought to himself.

In the third frame was a photo of the family at Disney World. It put on display for the world the love shared by the three members of this family. The trio of pictures appeared to be the only reminder she had of her family.

As the agent studied the pictures, rays of sunlight streaming through the window jarred her from sleep. When her eyes opened, she found Adam sitting upright next to her, leaning against the headboard, and studying her sleeping form. Looking at the clock she saw it was 8:30 am. Puzzled by his gaze, she asked, "Did you sleep at all?"

He nodded his head yes, but remained silent. She sensed his mood had changed from fun and silly to somber. Joni was unsure of what to make of the transformation. She had no way of knowing the short time he had spent with her had produced a sense of restlessness and dissatisfaction with his life.

She rolled over, placed her feet on the floor and left him sitting on her bed. He closed his eyes and listened to her padding down the hallway, headed to the kitchen. The sounds of her making coffee was his serenade as he made his way to the bathroom.

They sat at the kitchen table drinking coffee and talked. Joni found herself prolonging the banter by extending her answers with many details, to remain in his company. This was a new place for her. It had been several years since anyone was present to discuss her day, ideas, and feelings. Today, she was sitting with a fine specimen of manhood. After so many years of abstinence, many wild thoughts played in her imagination.

The aroma of the rich, dark soil and the warmth of the sun on his back was a revitalizing feeling for him. He was sneaking peaks at her shapely legs and noticed they were turning a light pink as the day progressed. Adam also noticed sometimes when she stretched a little too far above her head, he could see the scar on her thigh, recalling her many injuries from the accident so many years ago.

She had prepared him verbally for the antiquated tiller, but he was still surprised that it took all his strength to get it started. He wondered how she ever managed it on her own. When he finished turning the soil and mixing fertilizer into the rich dirt, he turned the tiller off, pleased that he had been able to finish the task for her. It seemed natural for the couple to stand side by side as they admired the totality of their accomplishments. Joni occasionally looked at him as she thanked him repeatedly and suggested he had done enough for the day. Her words attempted to send him away.

Anticipating his thirst, Joni had rushed out with some ice water and offered to make a fresh pot of coffee when the tiller fell silent. She was going on and on, worried that she has inconvenienced him with her gardening, to which he reminded her it was he who had offered, she had not asked. After he refused a third time, she insisted on preparing lunch as repayment for his labor.

Joni observed him and smiled when she accepted his outstretched elbow as he escorted her into the house. Adam found the touch of her hand on his arm as heady as any drink he had ever partaken. Together they prepared a lettuce salad with grilled chicken breast and lemonade tea. With such beautiful weather, they decided to carry their plates outside. Joni commented on how the azure blue of the sky was dotted with specks of fluff. From the shade of the patio while relaxing on the reclining chairs, they admired their efforts of the morning. Bandit quickly learned to hang out on Adam's side of the table because he was sneaking him scraps of chicken.

The tender seedling pots and packets of seeds were carried outside after the dishes were deposited in the sink. Adam found himself enthralled with the secret beginnings visible in the containers she carried outside. She shared there were many vegetables which could be planted in April. They spent the afternoon working in the sunshine, enjoying the feel of the warmth of the dirt between their toes, working side by side while hoeing the rows. Together they planted onions, potatoes, peas, broccoli, cabbage, lettuce, and spinach.

After the seeds were buried, she used small sticks as markers for the rows. Adam commented she must have a fine memory, but she explained that the plants looked different when they grow. She assured him once you were familiar with plants, they were easy enough to identify.

A small dogwood with its blossoms of white stars near the back of her property caught his eye. The agent decided her yard reminded him of her house, attractive, orderly, but not personalized. Flower beds edged with red bricks ran along the inside of the picket fence, softening the view. In some places violets had sprung through the patches of leaves and their purple beauty glistened in the sunlight. Red, orange and yellow tulips were waiting to bloom. But as his gaze lingered, he also noticed the flower beds were filled with debris and leaves.

"It looks like your flower beds need some TLC too." Adam remarked after assessing the yard.

"Are you a glutton for punishment or are you a slave driver like this at work too?" She laughed when she answered, while wiping her brow.

"A glutton for sure. I offered my assistance to free some of your time up later in the week. I am hoping we can get together again, soon. Come on, quit burning daylight," He cajoled, pulling her hand, dragging her into the yard.

Working together, it didn't take long for them to finish the yard work. "Wow! Now that is a yard to admire," she proclaimed proudly as she patted him on the back. The backyard was free of leaves, limbs, trash and weeds. It wasn't enough that he had helped with the vegetable and flower gardens, but Adam also mowed the grass as Joni used the weed eater to edge the flowerbeds and around the house.

It was now 5 p.m. Adam had only consented to one rest break since lunch time, so she insisted they call it a day. It had been a milestone day for each of them. Not just the amount of work that had been accomplished, but the ease of being with someone new. Both were shocked by the comfort they found in silence and the sensations felt every time their bodies made contact. Their touches were electrifying.

Both were sweaty dirty from the work and wet from watering the garden. It was a reluctant agreement not to share dinner together. Her hand naturally reached for him and was in the crock of his elbow as they made their way to the front of the house. Joni leaned slightly on his arm when she thanked him for all his help. She insisted on preparing dinner tomorrow night, if he was interested and available. She suggested a meal of steaks on the grill, a bottle of wine, and a bit more time admiring their efforts of today. It would be a wonderful way to spend a Sunday evening.

The agent agreed because the dinner invitation gave him a way back in, but the man agreed out of pure desire to be in her company again. "You are quite welcome, but remember, I am the one who wanted to spend the day with you. You gave me fair warning last night about what the day would entail. I just want to remind you I could truthfully tell others we slept together on our first date, you know, if I were a kiss and tell kind of guy." He said quite sarcastically, amused with his own humor.

"Well, I guess that is true. But then I'd have to let them know you were taken at gunpoint!" She laughingly snapped back at him.

After her shower, she rambled around the house. Joni found herself feeling grateful it held no shared memories of Jake. No one had delighted in anything within the walls of this house, including herself. But somehow guilty feelings rose, running counter to the giddy excitement of seeing Adam again. The two emotions played tug of war with her heart and mind until both were too exhausted to fight off sleep any longer. It all reaffirmed for Joni that she was alive and beginning to wade into the pool of the living. For the first time in six years, she had not prayed for the day to come to a close.

9.

Sunday was a beautiful spring day. People were throwing open their windows, clothes were being hung on lines, and lawnmowers could be heard on almost every block. The driveways of many homes were busy with kids playing basketball or cars being cleaned. Tulips were beginning to bloom, trees were filled with buds, and everything was turning green again. It was the evidence as to why this is called the season of renewal.

He made a pit stop at Clarks Feed Store on Big Bethel Road before driving to her house. Adam described for the clerk exactly what he was hoping to find. The old guy in bib overalls pointed to the aisle where the garden markers were kept. Unfortunately, there were only a couple of choices. The decorative ceramic stakes suit her style better, but they didn't have one for each kind of vegetable they planted. The metal stakes are less ornate, but there is one for every variety of plant.

A quick stop for wine was necessary too he decided. The wine shopkeeper recommended a dry red wine to go with steak, but he elected to go with a light, sweet Zinfandel. He remembered how she liked her coffee and figured it would probably be a safe bet for wine as well.

The minute she got home from work, Joni raced into the house and laid the steaks out on the counter thinking they need to come to room temperature for the marinade to get the most flavor into the steak. Outside, the grill was fired up so it would be screaming hot for a good sear on the steaks. Back inside, Joni scrubbed a couple of potatoes, wrapped them in foil, made a tossed salad, and lingered at the back door with Bandit when a vivid mental imagine of Adam without his shirt sneaked back into her thoughts.

Choosing clothes for the evening seemed to be the most difficult decision she had made all day. It had been years since she had given thought to her attire, wanting it to appeal to someone else. Flipping hangers from side to side, she finally spotted a pair of soft green capris, a white short sleeved v neck, cotton t-shirt. Then she ran a hair brush through her hair, pinched her cheek for a little color, checked her mascara, and then decided to go barefoot.

Adam pulled up at the curb promptly at 6 pm. Joni was watching for him from the kitchen window. Again, today he took her breath away. She found him the most handsome man she had ever seen in person. His faded denim jeans made his legs look a mile long and the yellow polo shirt emphasized his bronze color skin. He swung open the storm door when she called to him. Bandit was the official door greeter when he stepped inside. When he caught her gaze, and dazzled her with his beautiful smile, Joni became giddy with delight. In each hand, he was carrying a bottle of wine. It would be a relaxing night for sure she found herself thinking. When he reached the kitchen, the smell of his cologne arrived just before him. Joni recalled it was the same scent she had smelled on her pillows last night.

He chose wine glasses from the hanging rack, poured two glasses, then handed one to her. This is the third time he has taken charge in the kitchen she realized. Then the notion that Adam was already comfortable in her house, ran through her mind. After he complimented her outfit, he picked up the potatoes wrapped in foil and grabbed Joni's hand leading her into the back yard. He threw the potatoes on the grill then led her to the vegetable garden.

Adam was still enthused while looking over the newly planted garden and manicured lawn. The grass seemed greener, a few more flowers had bloomed, and the vegetable garden soil was dark and rich. The plants in the garden are standing tall, not wilting. He handed her a small brown package with the engraved, metal stakes. Carefully each stick was replaced with a clearly labeled metal stake. His gift brought profuse 'thank you's' and 'you shouldn't have's' as she fingered them.

The aroma of steaks on the grill filled the air as they enjoyed watching the sunset slide into the Chesapeake Bay from the patio. It was a spectacularly colorful show, as the streaks of pink, orange, yellow, aquamarine and blue of the sky mingled like melted color crayons, as the large red ball dipped lower and lower. Adam felt the display was more vivid and opulent because the experience was being shared. How wonderful it was to find happiness in some of the simple pleasures of life again he thought to himself as he observed the woman sitting across from him.

Once the dishes were loaded into the dishwasher and the kitchen back in order, Joni extended an offer to share a favorite place with him. It was so easy to be in his company, Joni sought ways to keep the night from ending.

After an exquisite simple supper, she invited him to a place she considered special, so without hesitation, he responded positively. The agent would go with her. Adam thought he couldn't remember the last time he had let his guard down and actually relax and have fun.

"Great, I will drive. My car already has everything we are going to need. Let me grab my shoes and keys and then we'll be off." She went bouncing from the room when he agreed.

Adam is familiar with this area and became concerned about her destination when she crossed the Monitor Merrimack Bridge. They were leaving Newport News for Chesapeake. She turned on a country road, which came up quickly after crossing the bridge. About a mile down the dark, gravel road, she pulled her vehicle over and brought it to a stop. Shit, it is pitch black on this road and there are no buildings nearby, the agent noted.

Joni had a huge smile when she cut the engine and the headlights. She also could see a funny look on his face, illuminated by the dome light, when she opened her door. Still she kept the secret. From the back of the car, she pulled out a blanket, a flashlight with red crepe paper taped over the light, and a disc shaped chart. His befuddled look became more perplexed when he examined the materials she handed him. As he fingered the items, his expression made her laugh out loud.

First, the blanket was spread on the hood of the car. Adam assisted her climb by holding her hand. She was radiant as she smiled at him from the hood of the car. Joni looked into the sky and announced this was her favorite spot to gaze at the stars. It was the first time she had brought anyone here or even asked anyone to accompany her.

Adam thanked her for believing he was worthy enough to share her private spot. But he had a surprise of his own planned. He extracted the second bottle of wine and two glasses from the backseat, then joined her on the hood.

They sipped the Zinfandel wine while Joni showed him how to use the star chart to locate stars with the crepe paper covered flashlight. She pointed out the North Star, Pegasus, the three stars that form Orion's belt, Hydra, Cepheus, Draco, the 'W' shaped formation that is the throne of Cassiopeia, Leo, Cancer and Ursa Major and Minor, or the big and little dippers, to name a few. He was astounded at the beauty of the black night sky filled with infinite twinkling lights. Although Adam said he had noticed stars, it had never been a purposeful pursuit. Before the evening was over, he confessed from this moment forward, every time he looked into the night sky, he would think of her.

They lingered at her hideaway spot for about an hour. Each viewing the stars, naming the constellations as they identified them, and sipping wine. Finally, they were just leaning back, resting against the windshield, not looking for anything when a fireball shooting star, with a long fiery tail, shot across the dark sky. They looked at each other and smiled, commenting it was a fitting ending to another perfect day.

It was at that moment Adam bravely asked if she would see him again. Then he suggested they spend many more days together, requesting Joni be his teacher, leaving the subjects up to her imagination. The look in his eyes was positively scandalous, as he took her hand in his and gently squeezed. The current that passed between them, caused each of them to shutter.

Jefferies decided he had been given an impossible assignment to complete. Right then he knew that this was invitation was no longer about an investigation, but just plain desire. Though he was cleared for any type of operation, including assassinations, he was unprepared for her.

He felt happy for the first time. New sensations were felt when he was with her. The agent realized more than anything he wanted to feel those sensations, well and to help make her smile again.

10.

The couple's desire to spend more time together was mutual. After comparing work schedules, they were distraught to discover they would be on opposite shifts for the entire week. It was impossible to reschedule to get them time before the week-end.

Adam called her every day and through each conversation Joni could visualize his radiant smile. The wall around her heart began a leisurely melt each time he let her name roll off his tongue. How excited she got when he sent a couple of texts to say he couldn't stop thinking about the next time they could be together. He admitted to her she was all he thought about these days. Certainly, he was not following the topic of the meetings he was attending.

Adam found himself obsessed with everything about Joni. Her subtle perfume, her sapphire blue eyes, her timid smile, her gentle touch, and his powerful desire to experience all of it again filled his mind. The agent felt their personalities were suited for each other and believed she too was appreciating the unexpected developing relationship.

Because it wasn't in his nature to wait, he created an opportunity for them to be together. On Wednesday morning, his patience was exhausted. He decided to surprise her with a picnic over her lunch hour. First Adam texted Joni to find out if she could get away and if so when. The recluse jumped at the chance see him again, so she promptly texted back 'yes at 11.' A response popped right back requesting her presence at the park across the street from the library. Once the time was confirmed, Adam called Marie, his housekeeper, and ordered a spectacular picnic lunch to be delivered to the park before 11 am.

Marie cursed him, stating all good things take time. Using his most authoritative manner, Adam reminded her she is paid well and he expected a wonderful lunch in two hours.

Sheer ecstasy was pumping through Joni's veins after accepting the lunch date. Everyone at the library must wonder what kind of pill she had taken, because suddenly there was a dopey grin plastered on her face. At lunchtime, she hurried to the meeting place, impatient to see his smile again. Secretly hoping to feel the touch of his hand against her skin. Joni went sprinting across the street, but skidded to a stop when she caught sight of him, feeling foolish that he caught sight of her running. Then she renewed her trek across the street, making her way to the man that created the butterflies in her stomach.

Adam saw her sudden stop and was afraid she had doubts when she stared at him. The pause was only momentary because almost instantly she wowed him with her genuine warm, wide, welcoming smile. He greeted the woman several feet from the table, eagerly confessing he had a surprise for her. When he stepped to the side, Joni could see a picnic table covered with a red and white linen tablecloth. On top of it was a picnic basket full of crystal stemware and china plates. He invited her to sit at the table and took charge of serving the meal. Oh, the delectable food that he pulled from that basket. There was a divine chicken salad with grapes and pineapple chunks, a small loaf of freshly baked Italian bread, a chunk of Havarti cheese, and slices of blueberry cheesecake for dessert. Adam admitted that Marie had truly out done herself, especially on such short notice, and given his high-expectations.

Their talk was mostly about practical affairs, such as the bull market, the forecast for the week, the rising price of groceries, and even high-speed railways found a way into the conversation. It was a sensible chat until he offered a toast, 'to afternoon delight' and clinked glasses with her. She thoroughly debated with him the inappropriateness of such a toast at a picnic lunch. Adam's eyes twinkled with mischievousness as he argued that she was completely focused on the here and now. That her imagination had not yet allowed her to explore the endless possibilities that exist when they get together.

Before her lunch hour was over they arranged to meet Friday after work, both too anxious to wait one more minute. Of course, they continued to talk every day. He delighted in the happiness he found in the time spent talking to her. Adam caught himself calling her to see if she was watching the sunrise, then later the sunset. The agent discovered that his selfishness with her time was easy to overlook when the happiness of the circumstance was reciprocated. Mostly Adam wanted to chat so he could hear her smile. Her smile of pleasure came across loud and clear, even over the phone.

When Friday finally arrived, Joni was mentally struggling to make it through the day without tears. Somehow being with Adam had helped her forget that today was the day. The seventh anniversary of her car accident. Or more accurately, it is the seventh year she has been alive without Jake and Jack. Her life was changing. Joni's heart was beginning to hunger for love again. The vivid memories of her life with Jake was fading. New and blissful memories were being created with Adam Carmichael.

Joni was not able to focus on any task she attempted and was tearful while on the library floor. She felt fortunate her boss was sensitive to her state of mind when she shared the reason for her emotional chaos. After giving her a hug, her boss allowed her to leave long before her shift ended.

She chose not to alert Adam to the change in her schedule, desperate to see him again despite the anniversary. Joni believed she could pull herself together before he arrived. The extra hours allowed her to change her menu for dinner. He wasn't to arrive until 8, so she busied herself with laundry, dusting, and vacuuming the house. Anything to keep her mind occupied with something other than Jake and Jack was the sole goal. Just making it through this day.

Adam showed up right on time in a pair of jeans and a button-down jean shirt. Even though she was emotionally distant, his smile invited her into his life. Once again, Bandit was there to greet Adam at the door. But this time she did not join him. Joni remained in the kitchen.

The agent's brain went into high gear as the aroma of delicious food hit him when he walked through the door. It was obvious as he entered the house, by the sights and smells, she had gotten off work early, but failed to extend an invitation to share the extra time with him.

Adam acknowledged she looked pretty. Already he could smell her Beautiful perfume, the scent he had come to know as her, as he approached the kitchen. Joni quietly greeted him as she continued to set the table for two and then served up some of the best ribs he had ever eaten. The agent instantly recognized tonight's atmosphere was entirely different from recent days. He complimented her on being a very good cook and thanked her for this special meal, but she remained mostly silent.

Something was wrong, but he just couldn't put his finger on it. She smiled in all the right places, but she barely participated in the conversation. In fact, it appeared she may have been crying, because her eyes were swollen. She had been on the verge of tears most of the night. But she wasn't sharing. Adam's mind raced through the events of the past week for any possibility of an answer.

Joni recognized once again that she was in the presence of a great conversationalist, but even he was having difficulty extracting conversation from her tonight. She could feel how hard Adam was working to keep the chit chat going, but she could barely manage a word in response. It was unfair to let him carry the entire conversation. Maybe it had been a mistake not to cancel when even the anticipation of the night hadn't lifted her from her sadness.

Finally, after pushing food around her plate and leaving asked questions unanswered, she found her voice. She accepted the blame for not being good company. But rather than disclose what was on her mind, Joni suggested Adam leave, admitting she was poor company. Adam shook his head no, emphasized with a look of dismay.

Always an investigator at work, Adam refused. He wanted to know more. Something was amiss and he needed to know what, if he was going to help her. After dismissing her request for him to leave, he rose from the table and began clearing away the dishes. Joni followed his lead and began opening containers for the leftovers. Adam left her to her thoughts and started washing dinner dishes. He had his back to her when she timidly asked a question.

Not only was her mind filled with grief, her body was filled with an overwhelmingly sense of utter aloneness. Isolation and loneliness had been her life for many years, but it was excruciating painful tonight. There had been no one to hold her, no one to talk to, and no one to love since Jake left her behind. Joni was embarrassed at her ache and intense desire to touch and to be touched by Adam. The longing was compromising the evening. Joni drew in a deep breath, fearful of being rejected, but the words slipped out before she could stop them.

"Could I ask a favor of you?" Her eyes were focused on the floor. She could not look at him, fearful of his answer.

"Of course." He replied still facing the sink.

"I'm so… may I touch you?" She shrugged her shoulders as the mumbled request escaped.

Adam turned from the sink to look at her, startled by the request. "Of course, you may touch me. In fact, I would like very much for you to touch me." He answered, not sure of what she was asking.

Joni lifted her eyes briefly. Just long enough to observe a baffled look on his face. The profound embarrassment of her request remained intact and was apparent in the blush on her cheeks. But the humiliation could not conquer her desire; it did not stop her hands from seeking out his body.

Her shame prevented her from looking at him. Keeping her eyes downcast even while her hands grasped his shirt. Joni started by tugging his shirt out of his jeans and then cautiously began feeding the bottom button through the hole. Painstakingly slow, she labored through each button without looking at him, careful throughout the process not to touch his skin. Her gaze rising ever so slightly as her fingers moved up the shirt. When she reached the final button at the top of the shirt, Adam placed his index finger under Joni's chin and gently raised her face, so she was looking at his face. There she found a look of compassion, mingled with concern.

"You were very quiet during dinner tonight and now this. What is going on Joni?" He whispered but did not stop her from pushing his shirt back, exposing his muscular chest.

If she spoke to answer his question, the floodgate would open; tears would fall relentlessly. Joni paused, managing only a passing glance at his face. When she recognized the depth of his worry, her eyes filled with tears. She was not sad and she did not want to cry tonight. Just wanting, no, needing to be held, was her earnest desire.

Joni broke off the gaze, focused only on her physical need. It was the last thing she wanted him to know about her, but he seemed to already understand. Cautiously she placed just her index finger over his heart, delicately touching his skin.   His heartbeat was racing under her touch as she next gently rested her palm in the same place. She never answered his questions.

But the tear sliding down her cheek was all the confession he needed. Then the man remembered. He stood over a hospital bed and helped plan funerals in April. His hand came up and softly rested over hers, not to remove the hand, but to caress it. "Please Joni, tell me what is wrong." He stared at her face closely and saw plainly what she was trying to hide. "I want to touch you too. May I?"

Joni could only manage to nod a yes to the question. Her body was filled with torment. Regardless of the valiant effort to hold them back, the tears broke free as she felt life and warmth under her fingertips. These tears were a mixture of loneliness and a burning desire to be touched. Not a sexual desire, just a pure need for physical contact.

She surprised him by quickly stepping forward, closing the space between them. Resting her chest against his. Her head rested on his shoulder while her arms reached around, under his shirt, pulling him close, rubbing his bare back with her hands. Adam felt her need and placed his hands on her shoulders, then began to stroke her upper arms. Up and down, caressing her skin. His hands stroking her neck, then his finger touched her cheek.

She was shaking her head no, rather than using words. Joni's breathing became rapid as she slowly and methodically moved her hands through the hair on his chest, feeling the skin beneath it. It was so sensual just to touch a man.

Adam lifted her shirt to touch her skin, but the action caused her to pull away. She stepped backwards, out of his reach. Her head was now fiercely shaking no as she found her voice. "Please don't do that. I am scarred and ugly. I can't figure out why are you here with me? YOU are so beautiful." Her voice was filled with anguish.

"Stop that! Let me look." He demanded, but then lowered his voice. "Please honey, let me see you."

Adam reached out for her hand and hauled her close to him, then began to lift her shirt again. When she did not object, carefully he continued. Once the shirt was over her head, he slowly spun her around to look at the scars. He remembered what they had looked like before and was amazed how well she had healed. There were only a couple of scars noticeable.

"Your imagination is playing tricks on you. These are far less obvious than you think. The plastic surgeon did excellent work." He reassured her. Tenderly Adam ran his hands up and down her back, across her shoulders and down her spine a few times. Afterwards he planted a kiss on the back of her neck. She spun around and clung to him as she broke into body racking sobs.

Adam guided her to the floor so he could hold her in his lap. They sat, her in between his legs, chest to chest, silently stroking and cuddling each other's torso. Joni embraced him as if her life depended on it. The sensation of his skin, the contact of his hands on her body, the tenderness of his gaze, and his reassuring words, had released the floodgate of pent up emotions. Now the agent felt he had the honest answer as to how she really survived the accident.

"Oh, Adam." she whispered in his ear, through the final tears.

But the words she actually said were, "Oh, Jake."

Adam held her till her crying subdued, and then he went on holding her, because that is all he wanted to do. Hold her for the rest of his life. He knew this night changed their lives forever.

It seemed like the lights came on as her tears subsided. The realization of the newness of this relationship with this man jumped to the forefront of her mind. Embarrassment caused her to make a queer sound in her throat as she began pulling away from him. She was stunned he had easily yielded to her need for physical contact. Joni turned abruptly, self-conscious by her appearance. She snatched her shirt off the floor and quickly covered herself.

Adam slipped his arm from around her shoulders, looked at her longingly, stroked her cheek with his index finger, and then looked down to button his shirt   It might have been the guilt from walking away from her years ago, or maybe knowing how truly alone she has been for so long, but suddenly Adam mentally committed to make her happy and to possess all of her, forever.

Adam cautioned her, "Its best that I leave now. I want to keep touching you…all over your body. We both know it's not the right time for that to happen." He tilted her head back and planted a long but gentle kiss on her lips.

11.

Adam called first thing in the morning and asked to see her again. She was grateful the events of last night seemed to have slipped his mind. Nor did her psychotic break seem to have driven him away. Unfortunately, Joni shared she had committed to a previous engagement. Sylvia's bachelorette party. She was obligated to attend because she was the designated driver. Joni explains though her yearning to see him is strong, she won't bail on her plans. They are co-workers and her absence would be noticed.

Silently she cursed herself for missing a chance to be with Adam. She questioned why she ever agreed to these things because they are never pleasurable for her. She understood the invitation came purely from an office politics requirement. Thank goodness, she had enough wisdom to bring a book. Joni located a large table at the back of the place, with plenty of light to read by, so she was set for the evening. Most of group was dancing, but Joni remained behind to guard the purses.

At 8:30 pm Adam had dressed and was headed to Norfolk via a limo. This was just another avenue to get to know the woman who occupied his mind 24/7. He used the excuse it was just a part of an investigation as he plotted to be near her again. Once the limo entered Norfolk, the driver told him the traffic on 42nd street was extremely heavy so they would be later than his anticipated arrival time. When the car finally turned the corner, they found the parking lot packed. The Wave was at capacity tonight.

Once he strolled inside, he immediately spotted her. Joni sat alone at a large table with her back against the wall with her eyes downcast. After her episode last night, this concerned him at first. Yet after carefully studying her form, Adam realized she was reading a book.

As he studied the object of his investigation, he committed to memory she was wearing a black and white print sundress with black sandals. Her hair had curls with one side pulled back in a sparkly clip. Joni looked pretty, but she sat alone, reading a damn book in the middle of a busy nightclub. Fury built in the pit of his stomach at the thought of such a vibrant woman sitting alone.

When the music ended, he observed several women gather at her table. The agent recognized some of the women from the library, so at least her reason for turning him down was truthful. They are laughing and telling stories, excitedly waving their hands all around. Joni barely lifted her head, but she nodded in agreement. Adam quickly realized she was not attentive to the conversation, not really a part of the party.

Lydia and Celeste discussed some wildly attractive man sitting at the bar. Though she didn't look up, Adam crossed her mind when she overheard the conversation. They would never believe she was keeping company with a very handsome bachelor. Knowing Joni and her way of living, it was just too far-fetched for anyone to believe, herself included, she thought.

A waitress came by their table, took drink orders, and then made her way to the bar. Adam noticed they didn't even make sure Joni had a drink. The DJ fired up the music again and couple of guys went to the table and enticed two of the girls onto the dance floor. Those left behind walked in a pack in the direction of the bathroom, leaving her alone once more.

His anger rose higher. Adam couldn't stand she was just sitting when she should be having the time of her life. Life was happening all around her and apparently, he was the only person aware of her presence. He continued to watch as her friends made their way back to the table but ignored her still.

Adam knew money influenced everything, so he decided to use it to his advantage. It was his turn to act. First a conversation with the DJ for a special request. The DJ first shook her head no, but a hundred-dollar bill in her hand swiftly changed the no into a yes. Then Adam weaved through the dance floor, making his way toward the table at the back of the room.

A couple of the girls watched as Adam sauntered up to their table. One girl looked at him and instantly offered her hand. Adam wagged his index finger no and pointed to the woman at the back. The girls looked at Joni, looked at Adam again, and then back at Joni. They were dismayed as they looked over at Joni one final time, to find she was completely unaware this god had shown up at their table.

She was so engrossed in the pages of her book, she hadn't noticed him. Finally, one of the girls uttered her name in such a tone that it compelled her to look up.

There it was! The smile broke out across her face when she saw him. Adam dreams about that smile and she was flashing it directly at him. He offered his hand to her, but she didn't move one iota. She looked at him and said softly, "I'm sorry. I am the purse guard tonight. If I leave these girls can't dance.

The man became furious again. Adam looked squarely at the young ladies at the table and started barking instructions. He looked at each woman around the table and informed them they will now be taking turns watching purses. Although they glared at him, the problem was solved for him. Joni was smiling when she closed her book, tucked it into her bag, then finally stood up, and moved around the end of the table.

"What are you doing here Adam?" she asked pleasantly, but looked at him from under her eyelids.

"Creating an opportunity to spend the evening with you. You said you would dodge this event if there was a way out, now I am going to provide you with exactly that." He revealed as they glided around the floor. Etta James was singing *At Last*, Adam's favorite song. It seemed especially fitting with Joni in his arms.

'My lonely days are over and life is like a song for me too! My life has changed. You are in it.' Adam was singing in her ear.

"Do you have any idea how much those girls are going to talk about you? Ordering them around and then asking to dance with me. Lydia mentioned earlier there was an incredibly handsome man at the bar. No wonder she was at a loss for words when you came to our table."

"I don't care about their gossip. I hate they take you for

granted. Put you in a corner and expect you to watch their purses. You should be out here dancing too, having fun. I have seen you seat dance in your car. I know you have some moves." Adam twirled and dipped her as they talked.

As he cradled her and lifted her back up to him, Joni face was flushed as she questioned him, "I agreed to do this tonight. It was my decision to watch purses, long before we met. But let me ask you this question. Would you like for me to be here dancing like this with someone other than you? Really?"

"Absolutely not. So, by coming here tonight, I solved my own problem." He chuckled, pleased with how the events of this evening were progressing.

" 'You're a good girl and you know it. You're exactly who you should be. Just hold on we're going home.' I AM taking you home tonight, you DO realize that?" He

138

was singing the words of the song into her ear. It was his way of informing her of his plans for the rest of the evening.

Joni's heart raced with anticipation, but she tried to explain to him, "I want very much to walk out of here with you, but I just don't see how your plan will work. Adam, I drove here tonight. I have to have my car in the morning, plus I have to get the girls home."

"I have thought of everything. I brought a limo here tonight. The driver has instructions to give your friends a ride home. I, on the other hand, will be riding with you. My truck is at your house."

Their conversation was momentarily interrupted by a young man tapping on Adam's shoulder. He completely ignored the man's request to cut in by shrugging the hand off his shoulder. He then informed the intruder the lady's dance card was full.

"A bit presumptuous don't you think, sir." Joni chided him, yet smiled at his boldness.

"Yes, it was indeed a gamble. One I was willing to take. I told you I wanted to see you. You said you wanted to see me, but this party was a problem. I say our problem is solved." Adam insisted.

She wasn't sure if he meant having the truck parked at her house or the dance card full comment was a gamble, but either way, she reveled in the knowledge he wanted her company and was fine with the entire world knowing it. She was aglow with excitement and thought herself one lucky woman.

When the final strains of music faded out, they strolled back to the table. The women had been keenly watching what they believed was a mismatched couple. They knew their meek coworker only as a homebody and loner, so they were particularly stunned she had her arms around such a hunk, at his request no less.

Joni thoroughly contemplated on the best way to introduce him to her work mates on the stroll back to the table. She settled on friend, because it was the truth. They weren't more than friends now. But she could let them insinuate anything they want from her statement.

Although his arm was wrapped around Joni's waist, Celeste invited Adam onto the dance floor with her. She would love to show him some real dance moves she advised as she gyrated her hips and reached for his hand. Joni knew from her Monday morning stories this invitation meant she'd move him right into the backseat of a car, for some extracurricular dancing if given the chance.

Thankfully he graciously declined indicating he had the woman of his desires in his arms.

The table went completely silent when he informed the group Joni was leaving with him, right now. Celeste's jaw dropped in shock from the announcement. He apprised them he had arranged for the limo outside to take them home. They could end their party whenever they liked, the limo was paid to stay until 2 am when the Wave closed.

She collected her bag and stood with Adam. The fact he had made travel plans for this group to get home told them he had come looking for Joni. They had a look of awe when he took Joni's hand, kissed it, and then lead her toward the door. She looked back and waved at them.

Outside, Ms. Crawford fished the car keys out of her purse and handed them to Adam. She suggested he drive, but perhaps he would be up for a moonlight stroll along the beach before heading home. He thought it was a great way to end the evening and pointed the truck in the direction of the beach.

Adam found a parking place at a closed business very near the beach. He hustled around the car to open the door. She was unfastening her sandals when he pulled the door open. The image of her legs wrapped around him popped into his mind but he shook it off. He knew that line of thought would make the rest of the night awkward. Next Adam shed his own shoes and socks and rolled up his pant legs, before they stepped in the sand and waded in the ocean waters.

Hand in hand, silently they waded along the water's edge, enjoying the sight and smells of the white sand beach. It was quiet, except for the sound of water lapping along the sand. The luminous moon was almost full and cast brilliant white and silver beams on the waves. The ripples of the incoming tide caused the reflections to break apart, scattering the shimmering beads of light as they washed upon the shore. They looked out over the ocean, watching the moon watch them. After strolling for several minutes in a comfortable silence, Joni tried to stifle a yawn.

"Oh my, I forgot about the paper route and how early you get up. Let me get you home." Adam insisted.

"I am tired. But I would much rather be right here with you." She assured him by squeezing his hand.

Adam stepped behind her and wrapped his arms around her waist. They stood with their feet in the water, as the waves lapped at their ankles and the tide eroded the sand under their toes. The moonlight was so bright so only a few stars were visible they commented almost simultaneously.

She clasped his hand and brought it up to her lips, kissed it and said, "Thank you, for saving me tonight…and last night. You are a good man Adam."

"I only wish I were half the man you believe I am, honey." He mumbled to himself.

Reluctantly, they turned back toward the truck. Adam tugged open the door and watched as she pulled her long legs inside and then tucked them under the dashboard. His plan was to peck her on the lips, but she deepened the kiss by lightly thrust her tongue between his lips. Adam groaned, then eagerly returned her sentiment.

12.

Vincent 'Vinnie' Gamble, was Adam Carmichael's

employer. Vinnie called an emergency conference of his

entire senior staff. He was ballistic about his front guy

missing and no amount of investigating had found him.

Breamer had been nurturing a relationship with a prince

from Saudi Arabia for many months. Although not in line

to inherit the throne, he apparently still had access to

unlimited funds. Breamer had been negotiating for some

very lucrative 'trade options.' What that meant in Vinnie's

world was money for weapons. Now the deal was dead in

the water because his negotiator had disappeared. Vinnie

was volatile and violent about his imagined financial losses,

throwing an ashtray across the room to emphasis his point.

Gamble declared during the meeting that

Carmichael was going in to salvage this deal and take

Breamer's place at the meeting in Chicago. Adam's head jerked up and looked at Vinnie. This was exactly the reason he was planted in this role, but this would be the first actual intelligence he could confirm about this specific negotiation. And Vinnie's decision for him to take it over.

Gamble continued there would be little prepping necessary for Carmichael, because the infrastructure had been laid by Breamer. Vinnie informed Carmichael he was assigning him this task because anyone in their business would know his reputation. Certainly, the prince has the intellectual capital that would generate a degree of comfort with the new negotiator.

The agent was instantly thinking about selfpreservation and planning for a safe drop communication.

To make the CIA aware of the impromptu trip to Chicago. His next thought was to include a request for his supervisor to make himself available. They had some personal issues to discuss and resolve. He knew Brett Wiegand would agree to meet because as a division chief, it was his job to assist the undercover agent.

In addition to keeping abreast of the agent's newest assignment with the Gambini family, an update regarding his investigation of Joni was long overdue to Brett. That was the portion of the meeting that would be unpleasant for both. Brett was not accustomed to Jefferies running a rogue operation. That was exactly what had happened with Joan Crawford, again. He smiled to himself as he admitted they had slipped into a comfortable daily routine.

Although they were not sleeping together, they were most headed in that direction. Over the past few weeks, Adam had an overwhelming desire to end the charade, which also meant ending his employment with the agency. He understood his usefulness to the agency in an undercover capacity had come to fruition. There was no doubt in his mind he would not be welcomed in an administrative position when he openly refused to follow orders. Failure to file timely reports, ignoring the personal involvement policy, and jeopardizing his cover again, would all be on Brett's list of complaints. Rightfully so, though Adam, solidifying his decision to part ways with both his employers.

Rather than focus on the meeting at hand, the agent found himself drinking and thinking about his future. Each day made him want to be with her more and he found he kept her company right up until time for her to go to bed. They enjoy watching TV, reading books, playing Scrabble or Rummy Cub, but mostly, they enjoyed being together. A bit of a rivalry was developing between them. She was ecstatic and did a happy dance when she defeated him, especially at Gin Rummy. Adam realized he was falling in love with the person he would now also identify as his best friend.

Joni had become his priority, his focus, the love

Adam unwittingly had been waiting his entire life to find. Somehow, through all the darkness of the undercover work, the lies, and deceit which had become his life, happiness found a way in. So much happiness that he found himself trying to avoid situations with risk, which would mean all work trips for Vinnie. Knowing about the devastating loss of her family, he wanted to be able to come home to her, always.

Gamble's rage continued into the wee hours of the morning, as did Adam's drinking. At 4:15 am, Carmichael drunkenly made the trip to Joni's home. When he entered, he was surprised to find her gone, but realized she was passing papers. He decided he needed to see her, to reassure himself this was real.

When Joni returned home, she saw Adam's truck parked at an odd angle and partially up on the curb in front of her house. She was so disturbed by the scene, she hurried into the house. There she found him on her bed, leaning awkwardly to the right, snoring loudly. First, she slipped off his shoes, then his jacket, where she was startled to find a shoulder holster and gun. Carefully she pulled the holster off and placed it on the nightstand. Adam mumbled as she tugged on him in an effort to make him comfortable on the bed. Joni grabbed his keys and moved his truck into her garage, leaving her car on the street.

When she returned to the house she found the man had rolled onto his side and sleeping soundly. She climbed in next to him and threw her arm over his waist and fell asleep herself.

Later, she felt him wake and tense under the weight of her arm. He did not move.

"It's alright Adam. It's me, Joni." And with that acknowledgement, she rose and left him in the bed.

He sat up and began fumbling for words. Before he could say anything, Joni knelt before him and placed her finger over his lips.

"Please don't explain. I now know you have your own demons. You wanted to be with me. Maybe because you feel safe here. Adam, I laid with you so you would know I will always have your back." With that statement, Joni left the room.

Adam was completely sober now, but bewildered by what he might have drunkenly shared. He had to consider the possibility – was she trying to tip him off that she knows his identity? Could she have sought him out, hoping they would send him in? Was their meeting accidental?

The agent rejected those thoughts as complete paranoia from being undercover too long.

13.

Adam instructed his secretary to purchase the best seats available and she did pretty well for such short notice. Front row was what he wanted for her, but the fifth-row center seats were sweet. Joni was very excited when he showed her the tickets for Luke Bryan and Marshall Tucker. He still didn't understand her love of that old country rock, especially since she listens to the current pop stuff now. But she absolutely knew the words of all the old country songs by heart. Bocephus, Conway Twitty, Travis Tritt, Johnny Cash, Merle Haggard, Willie Nelson, Waylon Jennings, and Dolly Parton. The oldies, but goodies she called them.

Arriving at the house ready for the concert, Adam wore jeans, boots and a baby blue polo shirt with a jean blazer. The blue of the shirt made his eyes and skin tone more intense than usual. The dark hair on his chest showed just above the open button on his shirt. His appearance caused her to catch her breath when he walked through the door.

Secretly, Joni wondered why he kept coming here to be with her, but prayed that he didn't change his mind about her any time soon. She thought about the budding relationship during the drive to Virginia Beach. Joni relished in the fact he took her hand and held it for the entire drive, absentmindedly rubbing his thumb back and forth across the palm of her hand. Even she recognized the transformation that was occurring. She was beginning to blossom, becoming human again under the constant attention of Mr. Carmichael. His affection and time gave her a confidence that she had not had or needed for the last few years. She had time to be herself, to learn about her likes, dislikes and preferences safely with him. He seemed to understand and tolerate her reluctance to rush into a physical relationship, but he let her think he was taking it slow too.

Her deep thoughts were interrupted as they were guided to their section by the usher. Once they had located their seats, rather than just sit and wait for the concert to begin, they took some time to check out the vendor booths. Adam surprised Joni and purchased a Marshall Tucker CD for his truck and a Luke Bryan CD for her. After cruising through the other vendors, they decided to stop for a glass of wine.

Adam was impressed. The Marshall Tucker Band had put on an excellent show. He found himself relaxed and smiling as he watched her have an enjoyable time. Joni sang and danced to all the songs, because she knew the lyrics to them. She had told him many times her favorite song by Marshall Tucker was Virginia. When she finished singing the lyrics directly to Adam, she whispered in his ear, "I want to be loved like that."

He affirmed her desire, "I think you have been honey, and will be again." On this night, she seemed young, vibrant, and carefree. This woman didn't resemble the one he met weeks ago. The one working then going home to a dog. Amazing what a little TLC could do for an injured person. The TLC worked on both of us, Adam thought.

At intermission, they decided to stretch their legs and get another glass of wine. Joni headed to the ladies' room while Adam waited in line for wine. While Joni waited for a stall to open, she took notice the exit was at the opposite end of the hallway from where she had entered. When she exited the bathroom, Joni looked around for Adam, but did not see him in the drink line. She decided to stay close so Adam would not have to search far for her in the throng of people.

As she waited in the walkway, a tall, bulky muscular man with stringy blonde hair, sporting a beard and moustache, rushed at her, slurring loudly, "Hey, I just saw you sitting on Carmichael's lap."

He positioned himself in front of Joni, blocking her way. Suddenly he grabbed her upper arms and shoved her backwards. His forceful action almost knocked her off her feet before he detained her by pinning her arms against the wall. The disapproval on his face was apparent as he looked over her body like he was selecting a piece of meat.

"You are a lot older than the gals he usually likes, but at least you got a nice shape. I wonder why he's been keeping you from me. Man, I can't wait to fuck you. I promise, I'll be the best you've ever had." The slurred words came from a face with a sneer and hot breath that reeked of alcohol. This man ground his pelvis against Joni as he spoke.

Afraid, but refusing to be intimidated, Joni pulled herself to her full height, stiffened her spine, and with all the control she could muster, asserted, "I seriously doubt that you are truly a friend of Mr. Carmichael. Based on your woeful lack of manners and your vulgar mouth, I can't believe you could even be an acquaintance of his." Joni pushed her entire body forward, trying to dislodge his hands. Then she continued, "But I'll share two interesting pieces of information with you. First, when I open my legs for a man, I'm making love to him. Only in your wildest dreams will that every happen between us. Secondly, if you don't take your hands off me this instant, I'm going to do it for you, and then you're really going to be sorry."

His look soured and his eyes went cold. Suddenly the volatility of the situation became apparent. His right hand released her arm, but only to be raised above her head. She realized he had every intention of smacking her. "You uppity bitch. I'll show you. Just who the fuck do you think you are?"

Before a plan to extract herself from his hold or how to avoid the impending slap came together, they both froze when they heard Adam shout, "Hey Sully. What the hell do you think you're doing to my girl?" Out of nowhere, Adam appeared behind the man.

Adam's voice obviously startled the man. The expression on his face changed and his hand dropped to his side like a piece of lead. Sully released her other arm simultaneously. The man stepped back, providing just enough space for Adam to place himself between the two. He possessively wrapped his arm around Joni, affixing her to his side, to prove to this man, as well as Joni, that she belonged to him and only him.

Luckily, this act caught Sully off guard. He knew

Adam not only as a lady's man, but as an abundantly talented hit man and the depraved reputation that went with the title. A man that would kill him right here and now, regardless of an audience. That knowledge alone forced him to cease and desist immediately.

"Listen carefully to my words, Sullivan. If you ever touch this woman again, if you look at her, in fact if I find out you ever say her name, I'm going to kill you, do you understand me? Or I promise you, my face will be the last thing you ever see in your life, got it! Now take a hike." Adam whispered his warning as he pushed his index finger in the man's face with hostility and absolute authority, sending the man on his way.

"Are you ok?" he asked thoughtfully as he turned Joni, checking her for injury.

All she could manage was to shake her head yes.

Tears rapidly filled her eyes, she refused to let them fall when Adam said, "Joni, we either need to leave and do this in private, or stay and pretend to enjoy the show. This guy wanted to intimidate you, but you stood up to him. He will be watching to see what effect he had on you and if he can use it against us in the future. I will do whatever you ask, but just know I will never leave you alone here again. You are safe with me." Adam swathed her in his embrace and whispered in her ear. She hastily regained her composure as she listened to his words. Tears disappeared as she shook her head yes. Joni clasped his hand tightly, leaned on Adam's shoulder briefly, and then agreed to let him lead the way back to their seats.

For all the wonderful things Adam had done for her and the patience he had shown, Joni knew she could be strong in the presence of ... what, an enemy? She was not sure who this guy is or how he is remotely connected to Adam, but the decision to stay at the concert was easy after she noticed he was again wearing the shoulder holster under his jacket. His threat to hurt Sullivan was real and he could indeed keep her safe.

Joni was preoccupied with her own thoughts while Luke Bryan performed. There were so many conflicting thoughts racing through her mind all at once. How could this well-educated, cultured, gentle, and caring man sitting next to her possibly know a thug like Sullivan? But it was obvious, they did indeed know each other from the results of the confrontation. What in their lives could bring them in contact? What do they have in common? She tried to imagine unimaginable possibilities from her isolated world perspective.

The trip from the concert to the house was made in an uncomfortable silence. Again, Adam took and held her hand, rubbing his thumb over her knuckles. Each were seemed lost in their own thoughts. Before she made her escape from his truck, he trotted around to open the door.

But instead of helping Joni out, he stood in the door and blocked her exit, keeping her seated in the truck.

"You were so quiet tonight. Please, let's talk about what happened at the concert." He begged, fearful the magic spell of a new beginning was broken.

Her head bobbed yes and no. Should she respond truthfully? "I was unbelievably scared. I've never encountered a man like him before. But then in an instant I felt safe with you at my side. Especially after I saw you were wearing your gun." Joni pointed at his left arm. There was a little break in her voice, exposing a brave effort to control herself and the whimsical bit of a smile.

Adam was discomforted by her child-like sureness in the disclosure. He also felt distressed as he glanced down at his shoulder, processing the words, and

163

comprehending where the finger was pointing. "Always observant, aren't you?" he stated proudly.

"It isn't the first time I've seen your gun Adam."

Not sure how to respond, he began, "I was around the corner standing at a table with our drinks when I heard his voice and realized it was him talking to you. You stood your ground with him, fighting your own battle. It wasn't until you told him to take his hands off you that I realized he was touching you. I would have come around the corner instantly if I had known he was threatening you."

She needed him to know she had felt in danger; a danger greater than she had ever known before. It was not only fear, but pain Sullivan inflicted on her. Joni shrugged the sweater off her shoulders to show Adam the bruises on her forearms. Purple imprints from Sullivan's tight grip were already present. Adam's face became flame red from his anger. "I'm going to kill him for hurting you." A new force swept over him. A sense of possession. He would fight at all cost to have this woman.

He stood outside the truck, leaning in toward her, rubbing the bruises on her arms, looking intently into her eyes when he made this declaration. Joni's hands cupped his face, then began stroking his cheeks. She thought momentarily before she asked. "Adam, who are you? Do you mean that figuratively or literally?" The quietness of the words left him speechless, though only briefly.

"You know exactly who I am. You have trusted me from the moment you met me. You let me in your bed right beside you, remember? The gun is part of my job, part of who I am. It does not change us in any way. At least I hope it doesn't." He watched her with pleading eyes. Nervous to hear the answer he added, "You are right though, it will be love making between us. I heard what you said to him. "

He was absolutely right. For some reason unknown to Joni, she instinctively trusted this man since the moment they met. She had indeed let a complete stranger crawl in her bed and then slept peacefully with him at her side. Adam was who she knows, who she wants to know better, and where she wants to be from this day forward. This really is an easy decision to make. To keep him in her life and to wait for them to mature as a committed couple.

What a turn of events he thought as he pulled away from her home. She was not and never had been a threat to him. Yet now he had become a threat to her and her way of life. Joni Crawford was now a complication in his life; a complication that will require close monitoring to keep safe.

Two days after the concert incident, Adam found himself on a 42-foot boat chugging through the Chesapeake Bay headed out to the Atlantic Ocean. The team of men were to meet up with another boat to accept delivery of some illegal merchandise for Vinnie. The traveling companions were Adam, Leo, Eddie and Sully. Adam chose to pilot the boat, meaning he could drive from up top, to keep his distance from Sully. He was still seething over the purple and green bruises on Joni's arms.

When the rendezvous coordinates were reached, the inboard motors were cut, the anchor was put out, bait placed on the lines of the outriggers, and then dropped over the sides of the boat. It is all a part of the deception. No real fishing was to happen, just a meeting. The three men below were drinking while they waited. Sully told his conquest stories, trying to be funny. He thought of himself as a gigolo, but Adam thought he was just an ass. When he heard Sully, mention running into "Carmichael and an older lady friend" at the concert, his reflexes took over. He flew down the ladder, pulled out his gun, and jammed it in

Sully's face. "I fucking thought I promised you I would be the last thing you ever saw if you mentioned her. Do you remember me saying that to you dumb-fuck?" His voice dropped back down into his throat and each word was weighed. The cool metal of the gun barrel pressed against Sully's forehead as Adam used it to walk him backwards, right against the side of the boat. There was a dead silence between them for a moment. The look on Adam's face appeared to be that of the devil.

"Come on Adam. It was just a joke. Hey man, she ain't like the girls you normally screw. I figured she must have something REAL good, you know, for you to date someone that old." He grinned, tossing glances between Adam and the others, as he tried to explain his way out of the mess.

"Well Sully, the joke is on you. She's is REAL good to me and she's going to be my wife." With that comment, he squeezed the trigger. The bullet ripped through Sully's forehead, thrusting matter out of the way as the bullet propelled through his brain and exited the back of his head. As his body rocked from the impact, Adam assisted his plunge over the side of the boat with a wellplaced kick to the center of the chest.

Leo and Eddie just stood, astonished at Adam's ferocious reaction to Sully's tale. To ensure their forever silence, Adam purposefully waved the gun in their direction and through raging anger asked if they had comments they wanted to share. Both terrified at the wrath just exhibited, shook their heads no. When he lowered the gun, they dropped back into their seats and went back to drinking, in total silence. Before he climbed back up the ladder, Adam threatened the two of them exactly the same way he had Sully. Don't say her name, look at her, or think about her, or he guaranteed, they would end up the same way.

14.

Part of their new routine was an understanding they would do the yard work on Friday evenings together. The warmth of the sun, the smell of freshly cut grass, the dirt between their fingers, and sharing the experience brought smiles when they worked in unison. It was one of the many simple pleasures of life that Adam came to appreciate while spending time at this house.

On this Friday, she had other plans in mind. She immediately got started on the outside chores after the paper route was finished. The goal was for Adam to have some down time. Joni made quick work of weeding and watering the garden. Typically, not one to start the mower before 9 am, today she worked quickly so that the yard was mowed, edged and trimmed by 11:30 am. Most of the flowers had come into bloom, so the flower beds got some special attention too.

This would be the perfect weather day to take the winter cover off and fill the pool. After all the yard work was completed, she took a well-deserved break before tackling the pool. The sun felt very warm on her face as she rested on a lounge chair on the patio. She was smiling inside about how all the hard work would allow her to have Adam all to herself the rest of the weekend. They could do whatever came to mind.

Joni and Bandit were nowhere to be found when Adam pulled up at 2. The windows of the house were open, so he knew she wouldn't have gone far. Glancing out the back door, he saw her stretched out on a lounge chair.

Quietly he closed the screen door to surprise her with his early arrival. Adam stood over this woman, gazed down upon her, and noticed how peaceful she looked when she rested. The fragrance of cut grass wafted through the air when a gentle breeze blew and directed his attention to the manicured yard. Oh, she was tired because she had been very busy, he realized. All the yard work was done and the flowerbeds and vegetable garden were in good order too he observed.

She mumbled as her head fell to one side. It was the mumbling that made him realize she was asleep. Joni looked so calm, so beautiful. As he admired her, he noticed the faint scar on her cheek was getting a little red.

The best thing about Joni was she was waiting for him. Adam was suddenly consumed with feelings of yearning that burst free as he stared at this woman. The potency of this longing was far greater than his strength and his determination to be with her was as vast as the sky. He knelt at her side, recalled their days together and unconsciously rubbed his finger up and down the scar on her cheek, which caused her to stir.

The tickling sensation caused her to swat at her cheek. When she batted at her face, she struck an arm. Then there was the soft pressure of lips against hers. "I'm so glad you're home Adam." she murmured, waking, but her eyes remained closed.

The words that fell from her lips hit like a kick in Adam's gut. "I'm so glad you're home Jake," was her actual phrase.

"Honey, it's me. Adam," he replied as he dragged his index finger along her cheek one more time. He whispered in her ear, "What are you doing out here?"

Joni mused because she had a surprise in store for him. As her eyes opened and she smiled up at him she chuckled, "I know it is you silly. I thought you deserved a break from MY chores. I want us to have time for fun."

Her left hand automatically went to her cheek, the exact place his finger stroked just moments before.

"Joni, please don't do that. I wish you could see the woman I see when I look at you?" He insisted as he pushed her hand away. "Even with this teeny little scar you are so beautiful. It is the events of your life that define who you are today. You are so innocent, not hard and angry, which would be quite possible after what you've been through. I think you are the most caring person and most beautiful woman I have ever met." Carmichael said with warm appreciation.

Her typical physical response when she could not reconcile words with actions was to shake her head. Right then she shook her head no. Her cheeks were ablaze from embarrassment. "Thank you for the compliment. But all I see when I look in the mirror are my hideous scars. They define how I think and feel about myself. Adam, why are you here? I'm forty-three years old with a body that is scarred and beginning to sag in all the wrong places. Since the accident, there is no chance of me having children, nor am I interested in adopting. I have no particular talent, nothing special to offer the world, so I hide. It's a wonder I met you at all. It makes me ask myself why a bachelor such as yourself would want to spend any time here with me. You are handsome, intelligent, articulate, charming and desirable."

She pointed out the facts as she believed and as honestly as she felt. He recognized the progress she had made, because despite her embarrassment, she kept her eyes focused on him. These details of her life were hard things for her to share. Before Adam, only the therapists and counselors had used kind and encouraging words, but none of their words had such an intimate feeling or meant so much to her.

Adam dragged another chair around and positioned himself directly in front of Joni. He lifted her feet from the ground and placed them in his lap, unlaced her sneakers, pulled them off, and began rubbing the soles her feet after stroking her calves a few times. After the touching incident in the kitchen, Adam tried to caress her and touch her each time they were together. She would never lack for human touch as long as Adam had anything to say about it. Tonight, a foot massage took place as she confessed her deep secrets to him.

He laughed at her biased description of him, but countered, "Thank you for that unrealistic assessment of Adam Carmichael. But your portrayal of me is not correct. I am fifty years old with a short, failed marriage in my distant past. I don't want children at my age. But where ever you are, is where I want to spend my time," he sternly continued as he rubbed her foot. "But I want to ask you something personal," he assessed her with a furrowed brow that Joni knew as concern.

As much as she trusted him, she hesitated, but then offered, "I don't know.   You ask and I'll decide if I want to answer."

It was the CIA agent who inquired, although he would no longer investigate her for the agency. "How DID you get the scar on your cheek? You seem self-conscious about it. It really is barely visible to others and I only noticed it more today because it is turning a little red in the sun, because I bet you don't have any sunscreen on, right?" ventured Mr. Carmichael.

Joni contemplated what she should tell Adam, which cause the color to drain from her face. There was a stir in her mood like a change in the tide. "Oh, Adam. I knew this day would come and I have dreaded the thought of it. This is very touchy subject for me, but you should know about me, the REAL ME and my life. So, you really know who I am." Her head shaking no, but the words came in a torrent. "Remember I told you my husband and son were killed in a car accident? Well, I was there. In the car, too. That's where the scars on my face and on my back, that's where they come from. The whole thing…the accident…it was my fault, that… we were on the road that day. I had seen an article about a new exhibit at the zoo and I insisted that we drive up to DC to the National Zoo to see the new pandas on exhibit. It was a beautiful spring day. Too nice to be inside, so I thought what a wonderful way to enjoy some family time in the fresh air. We had such a good day together. You know the kind of day you reflect on and think 'I'm so glad we made the time to do that.'

Jack had just turned 13 years old. He was just beginning to be embarrassed to be with his parents. In between a boy and a young man stage. On the ride home, my exhausted Jack fell asleep in the car. You know how a person's head kinda bobs around when they are sleeping sitting up? Well, I took off my seat belt so I could get him more comfortable…to lay him down in the back seat. Just as I got onto my knees and was reaching over the seat, a car driving like a bat of hell came from nowhere and sideswiped us. I could see Jake trying to maneuver the steering wheel out of the corner of my eye, but our car spun around just before it slammed into the guardrail. The impact caused me to be thrown from the car. From that point, I could only hear, but not see, anything else. The sound of squealing rubber and the vicious sound of metal on metal. I was told that after the car hit the guard rail, it flipped over the rail and then rolled down the embankment. I could hear sound of cars honking, but then it was eerily silent. Way off in the distance I began to hear voices. The next thing I could sense, well smell, was sickening stench of smoke."

Joni's voice cracked the instant the story had begun. Tears streamed down her cheeks. The mother choked on a lump in her throat when she spoke Jack's name.

She shook her head to regain her composure. "You know how you read about people getting a burst of adrenaline so much that, well, that they can lift a car off someone they love? Well, I didn't. I just laid there. I think I called out to Jack. I wanted him to know I was close, but I couldn't hear him answer. The next thing I remember was the hospital. The doctors said I had injured my back and suffered some brain trauma. There were numerous cuts and contusions, including the cut that caused this scar on my face. I eventually had surgery on my back. The trauma caused my brain to swell. Funny thing about all this, the doctors told me how lucky I was to have survived. I just kept thinking how moronic can they be? I lost my happily ever after that day. I was really lucky, huh." Sobs racked her body, as her hands hysterically waved all about her face, and her breathing was so ragged that hyperventilation was possible.

When Joni finally spoke again, she finished the story starting with an awkward laugh, "I laid in that hospital bed and missed everything. No goodbyes, no choices, no nothing. Someone planned the funerals, which I did not attend. When I was released from the hospital, I refused to go back to our home. Too many memories there. Which is how I ended up here, at this house. The only things I have left from my past are two boxes of stuff that someone thought was important enough to pack and my Bandit. I'm ashamed to tell you that I didn't save my family. I didn't even try!" she cried and her entire body shook with outrage.

Adam's strong hands reached under her arms as he lifted her from the lounge chair. He gently pulled her close to him as his arms clasped tightly around Joni's waist. She grabbed at his back, finding she could not get close enough to him. He continued to hold her, letting her bury her face in his chest, muffling the distraught sobs. Adam held her as he rested his head on the top of hers, stroked her back, and tried to comfort her. As the frantic tears receded, he lifted her into his arm and carried her into the bedroom. Adam sat on the bed, with Joni on his lap and held her in his in arms until her tears ran dry.

Adam was caught in his own thoughts as he held her. Thinking even with red eyes, swollen cheeks, and a runny nose, she was the most beautiful woman he had ever known. Why does she remember so much about the accident, but not him? What would happen if she remembered him? What will that revelation do to them?

Somewhere in the tearful sobs, she imagined she heard Adam whisper something about another chance at happily ever after. She was spent. Joni had been on an emotional rollercoaster, so Adam decided he would take care of fixing dinner. Mostly he wanted to stay with her, to hold her, to keep her fears at bay. To show her that he would be here through thick and thin. So, she could tell him she remembered. So, they could begin to deal with the collateral damage of his deception.

Joni clinched her eyes shut; fearful of what she might read in his expression. Would he feel the same contempt for her that she carried around for herself? But Adam just held her until her breathing got regular and her body relaxed enough to stop shaking. Gently he laid Joni on the bed, brushed some of her hair out of her face, and then placed her blanket over her body. Then Adam left, not just the room, but the house.

Joni heard his truck motor come to life and the sound of the engine faded away as it left the curb. The sound of the truck provoked her tears once again. She willed them not to fall. She mentally screamed at herself,

'I should have kept my mouth shut. You've scared him away. No one wants to be with a lunatic. It's been seven years! You should be over this by now!' But the tears were unrelenting from the past pain and now a newly inflicted wound. Sleep finally released her brain from its continued torture mantra.

Unfortunately, her brain found comfort in sleep for only an hour, then the hateful chant made its way back into her thoughts. Instantly she rolled off the bed and found herself back outside in the yard. Busy, mindless work was the best way to rid her thoughts of such negativity. She decided it was better to begin the familiar routine of being alone. No one could blame Adam for running away, especially not her.

While Joni worked outside, Adam arrived back at the house. He was nervous because Joni wasn't on the bed, nor was she in the kitchen. He turned on the oven and slide the casserole dish inside. The flowers and candles he snagged from his house were placed on the table. Then he headed outside to look for the love of his life.

Although Joni couldn't imagine using the swimming pool alone, it was a mindless task that would fill the rest of the day with busy work. Once she located the end of the cord that secured the winter cover over the top of the pool, the task of opening the pool began. First, she unfastened the cord from the lock that held it tight and in place, then pull the cord through the grommets that went all the way around the cover. Once that the cord was free, the winter cover was loose, it dropped into the water. Now it was free to be rolled back and removed.

It was a struggle to remove the tarp alone. Almost an impossible task in fact. Once Joni had muscled one side off half the pool, she began walking around to roll the cover back on the other half. She stopped in her tracks when she imagined she heard his voice. It sounded so real and so close it caused her to turn, to look for him. When she glanced up, she saw him on the patio watching her. "Hey, could you use a hand? I didn't think I was gone that long. I guess I thought you would sleep until I got back. I went out to get us some dinner because I did not want to wake you by making noise in the kitchen." He stood at the edge of the patio, with Bandit by his side. The V that formed between his eye brows when he was worried, lifted when he saw her.

"Oh, well I wasn't asleep when you left, just out of tears. I thought you left, you know, for good. I thought I scared you away." Joni mumbled in his general direction.

"Why? Because you hurt and you cried? Oh Joni. Surely you know me better than this by now."

"No way around it Adam. I'm scary. You know, too much baggage. And maybe because I'm crazy not to be past this after so many years. I still get so upset and emotional when I have a difficult day. And Adam, I do have them. This is the first one in a long time. I'm just sorry you were here to see me break down." She was frozen in place at the side of the pool and waited for his response.

"Look at me, Joni. I'm standing right here and I'm not going anywhere because of a few tears. What you told me about today was a horrific, life changing experience. Not something anyone should ever have to suffer through. I don't know how you have borne it all this time alone. You need to forgive yourself. There was nothing you could have done to help your family with a broken back, you realize that, don't you? Joni, you are an amazingly strong woman to have survived, both mentally and physically. I can't pretend to know what it feels like, but I think I'd be more worried if you didn't have tearful bad days. Joni, you loved them and they were your life. It is ok to miss themstill, even forever." He reached out his hand to her, but he remained in place on the patio. The future of this relationship rested on her next decision.

A relieved smile crossed Joni's face as she ran over to take his hand. His face registered relief as he pulled her close and enveloped her in his arms. She felt safe here. His arms felt like it could be home.

Adam joined her at the pool to help finish taking the cover off. They worked together folding the cover then stowing it away in the garage. He held her hand as he led the way back into the house. When they came through the back door, into the kitchen, Joni spied the table was set with flowers and candles. Somehow the most delicious smell was coming from the oven. As she looked around for more deviations from the normal, she also noticed a small, overnight bag sat beside the front door.

When Adam observed the puzzled look on her face, he told her. "It's not for you. I'm not carting you off to the funny farm today." he laughed at the look she gave him. He reassured her he had gone home to get an overnight bag. While he was there, he had his housekeeper pack up the chicken pot pie she had prepared for his evening meal. He was prepared to spend the night, only if it was what she wanted.

The rest of the day was spent together, but in relative silence. Even with the episode which had transpired between them earlier, it was still a comfortable silence. Neither was sure what to say next. Each was afraid of re-opening the gaping wound of her loss. They enjoyed a leisurely stroll along the Chesapeake Bay as they walked with Bandit after the tasty dinner.

Joni nervously consented to Adam staying overnight. The thought of him in her bed was exciting yet frightening at the same time. His touch, his smell, the way he was so protective of her was almost too much to imagine after believing he had left her.

As they prepared for bed, both wore pajamas when they turned in for the night. They smiled because they were thinking along the same line. This was just a shoulder to lean on, nothing more. She guessed Adam was fearful of another crying jag if the memories haunted her again tonight. Maybe he thought he would be a distraction for her. Once they settled in the bed, Adam rolled to his side to face Joni. He propped himself up on his elbow and stroked the scar on her cheek again. His touch was gentle, but it had an electric charge against her skin. He had no way of knowing the desire he caused to build in her belly, just because he touched her.

Adam pushed some hair from her eyes and stroked the other cheek and lovingly gazed into her eyes before he spoke. "I've been trying to think of something I could say to you that would take away all the pain and make you feel better. I even prayed to God to give me some wisdom or some magic words, but I realized there are just no words that release you from this pain. I understand why you suffer, but I hate that you blame yourself." His eyes became moist as he talked.

"Oh, Adam. I can't talk about the accident without falling apart, so I just don't." she reached out to caress his face. To acknowledge the sympathy, he was sharing. "I was so lucky because my life with Jake and Jack was filled with wonderful memories. Jake was a good man and he loved me well. He was a great listener, a better gift giver, and we were friends too. Ours was a very happy marriage and the Air Force provided a good life for us. Although I miss him terribly, unfortunately it isn't so unusual to bury your spouse, especially a military spouse. But no one can prepare you for losing your child. Ripping your heart out of your body might begin to describe the agony.

Jack, well my Jack. He was the light of my life; everything good. He was handsome, smart and had a silly sense of humor. He loved telling the most ridiculous elephant jokes. They weren't really funny, but his body language and delivery would make you crack up every time." The words just spilled out.

"Jake thought every boy should have a dog, but I knew regardless of the promises that he would take care of a dog, it really meant more work for me. I was completely against getting Bandit. When they brought him home, they ganged up on me. Insisting I should be the one to name him. I know they were thinking it would make me be happy about having a dog. And they brought Bandit home during the work week, so I had to care for him while Jack was in school. God knows they were 100% right. I fell in love with his gorgeous face and the puppy smell of his kisses. You know, I named him Bandit, not because of his markings, but because he stole my heart despite my absolute resolve not to like him.

Bandit and Jack were inseparable. It's only because we had traveled to all the way to DC, that Bandit wasn't in the car too." Bandit had come into the room when he heard his name. He spun around in three circles before he settled in his dog bed, which laid beside the bed. They both watched him and smiled.

Adam listened and watched her closely. "You have this special smile when you talk about them and your face lights up too. I can tell it was a very happy time in your life. But I see that same smile when you talk to me. It makes me feel incredibly special. It's unlike any feeling I've ever known, Joni. I can hear your smile on the phone when we talk. It's why I want to hear your voice rather than text."

He looked her straight in the face and said matter-a-factly.

His astute observation caught her completely off guard, yet after thinking about it for a minute, she realized he was right. She too could feel a physical change take place in her body, mind and spirit when he was part of the day. Happiness just flooded her entire person at the thought of Adam Carmichael.

Joni unknowingly admitted another new piece of information to the agent, "Do you realize you are the first person, maybe the first thing, I've cared about since the accident? You are the first person to step foot in my house on a social call. YOU are my only new memories. I've made so many with you and best of all, they are all happy. And the first one to touch me. I'd be lying if I told you I'm not scared. I'm not sure I can handle another relationship ending. My heart and brain play tug of war with the past and present. But our time together makes me feel alive. I'm not ready to let that feeling go. That is providing everything I said hasn't scared you away…you still want to be here."

"Look at me. I'm still here" he stared her right in the eyes pointing at his chest.

"May I ask you a question now?" Joni smiled that smile. Adam leaned in close to hear her question. They were side by side and nose to nose in the bed.

"Oh God. I'm not sure after our earlier Q & A session," but he laughed as he said the words.

"Would you kiss me like this from now on?" She asked as she leaned into him and claimed his mouth as her prize. Their tongues began a dance, their bodies pressed together, her fingers ran through the hair on his chest and he massaged her back.

"Wow," he said breathlessly, when they came up

for air.

That smile was plastered on her face as she handed him his blanket. She then took her own to cover herself as they laid side by side, each under their own blanket, holding hands as they fell asleep.

When the alarm went off at 3:45 am, Joni found it difficult to move. She feared something was physically wrong when her body did not roll over so easily. As she became more fully awake, she realized through the night, Adam had thrown her blanket over him and was spooning with her. His right arm had her pinned down at the waist. It was the most glorious feeling Joni had experienced in years.

The alarm had awakened Adam too. He could smell her scent, feel the bare skin of her leg against his own. His arm was draped across her waist and she was pressed against his chest. She was here because she belonged to him even in his sleep. He nuzzled her neck, sending a sensation through her body, creating an ache in the pit of her stomach. Knowing they are in a tenuous place, he gave her a quick peck on her lips, pushed away from her before she could feel his erection. Then he rolled over, jumped out of bed and ran off to the bathroom to get dressed.

Adam was becoming familiar with the radio station Joni enjoyed in the morning. It was high energy, alternative songs that provided some desperately needed motivation this early in the morning. He cranked up the volume as they sang and danced to Flo Rida, Katy Perry, MacLemore, and Rihanna, to mention just a few of the singers he was coming to know. Adam admitted he was still more a country song kind of guy, but he now knew some of the raps and sang most of the lyrics from Katy Perry's song, Dark Horse. He pointed directly at Joni when he sang

'Baby do you dare to do this, cause I'm coming at you like a Dark Horse' while thinking Joni had no clue how true those words were about him.

Adam had made a safe drop, to notify the agency about the trip to Chicago, and his new role as negotiator with the prince. Everything is confirmed, so it's time to tell Joni about the out of town trip. While they delivered the papers, Adam reluctantly shared the new of his out of town business trip. He disclosed he would be leaving in two days. This trip would last at least five days if all went well. It might be longer if he ran into unforeseen complications. He informed her it was the first time he could ever remember wanting to refuse a job-related trip. The challenge of solving problems was something he used to look forward to, but now the pleasures of every day home life with her made him happier. He would miss her more than he could describe with mere words.

Adam described a few details about his job. He started with the fact he worked for a man named Tony Gamble. Gamble operated several types of business endeavors and was considered an incredibly ruthless and unscrupulous businessman. Adam explained his official title of 'public relations representative' was quite deceptive, because the expectation of his duties was that more like that of a 'cleaner'. A fixer of messes. To find immediate solutions for deals that were problematic or falling apart. Resolving issues and conflicts that might lead to bigger problems if left unaddressed. Sometimes just his physical presence reassured everyone involved and things ran smoothly because issues got identified quickly. But sometimes, a real problem existed and a real solution must be sought.

Joni listened closely and thought it seemed he was trying to get her to read between the lines, but she shrugged it off as her imagination running wild, having read too many spy novels. But it was the most he spoken about his

job since the night of the Sully incident.

15.

When the plane made its bumpy touch down in
Chicago at 11 a.m., Adam hailed a taxi to get to the
expensive and luxurious Trump Hotel. Because
Carmichael was a regular here, no one was surprised during
the check in process he required a chauffeured vehicle be at
his disposal on a moment's notice.

At 4 p.m. Adam called down for the car and asked
the concierge about any new restaurants where he could get
reservations on such short notice. He pondered the choices,
made a selection, and then requested the man confirm a 7
p.m. reservation for him. When Adam exited the hotel
lobby, he found the limo at the curbside. Wiegand, decked
out in a chauffer's uniform, ran around and opened the door
for his passenger. Gramm's picture was on a placard on the
sun visor that read Driver in Training. It made Adam

chuckle out loud. Adam knew Gramm was always training someone new, but now he was the trainee.

The conference began immediately upon the closing of the limo door. He dispensed with formalities entirely because the very first question out of Wiegand's mouth was "have you followed orders? Have you ended the relationship?"

Adam smirked smugly because he knew he was going to thoroughly enjoy this conversation. "Do you want me to sit here and lie to your face? Because I'm sure you already know the answer to that question." he retorted. Wiegand fiercely shook his head. The back and forth movement made Adam think of Joni. "Are you purposely trying to end your career? And blow your cover at the same time?"

Jefferies leaned forward and looked at Wiegand

closely, wanting his full attention. "Yes, I believe I am. I have decided I am ready to be extracted from this assignment. If that also means the end of my career, then so be it. I have given everything to this agency for more than twenty years. Now I have found someone who accepts me and makes me deliriously happy. I'm wise enough to know what that means and I am not willing to let it slip through my fingers." In a single statement, he divulged the full extent of his feelings for Joni to the CIA.

"Leaving the agency! Over a woman. Are you fuckingkiddingme!? She is at the very minimum a…a …complication. Jefferies, surely you know there is no guarantee she will stay with you when she learns about this deception you have perpetrated on her for the past few weeks. Did you think about that yet?

Have you given any thought the harm to our operational security and the leads and information we lose if you are pulled? What happens if you are discovered because of her? If Gamble discovers your true identity because you have allowed yourself to go stark raving mad over a woman? What have you achieved for your life of sacrifice if you lose your life and possibly hers too?" This time Gramm threw in his two cents worth and tried to get the agent to reconsider this absurd decision.

Resting his head against the seat again, Adam grinned as his mind churned the possibility of a future with her. What living an ordinary life might be like for them. "Do you two have any idea what a perverted life we lead? Nothing we do is experienced by regular people. There is a real world of normal people and truly, we are not among them. Can you believe I was actually suspicious of Joni the night she took me star gazing? Because she took me into the country on a dark road. To see the stars better. Nope. Sorry, Sebastian. Right now, I don't care to think about anything but my own happiness. She makes me so very happy. And yes, I think she will understand. It is worth the gamble to me. I WANT OUT. Are you two listening to me?

You need to plan for my extraction from this op, because I am leaving. Please hear me clearly, if I don't feel like you are winding this operation down, I will find my own way out. I will commit to doing as much as possible to make this deal happen before I go. But by the end of the year, I am done. You do it or I will." Jefferies vowed. Somewhere deep down the thought of Joni being hurt crossed his mind briefly. If this decision was a mistake, the cost was too horrible to contemplate.

Gramm started to bitch and moan about his choices, sacrificing terrorist intel for the agency and blowing off a career. It seemed oddly personal for him, but Adam brushed the thought away in an instant. His mind was made up so he tuned Gramm's voice out completely. He would not hear any more discussion about his choices.

Adam understood Wiegand is furious he was still seeing Joni. Either she warrants investigation or she needs to be out of the picture. His opinion was she had become a distraction again, which made him completely ineffectual as an intelligence officer. Ms. Crawford may well be a threat to him and his legend if he isn't truly investigating her. It was a violation of agency policy to become involved with a suspect. Vinnie would use anything at his disposal to keep his people in line, meaning she could be used as a tool against him. And everything they listed was truthful and correct. Adam listened to their spiel but at the end of the day, he called her anyway. Just to hear her voice, just to make her happy. Hell, really, just to make himself happy. There was nothing anyone can say that would keep him from her.

He had ignored the rants and raves and the grim expressions that took place in the front seat, so he was scarcely conscious of where they were driving. Adam finally interrupted them by asking, "Are you ready to discuss the prince yet?" He tried to change the focus to the job at hand.

Sebastian threw his hands up in anger, which was dangerous since he was driving. The lengthy discussion about the prince was thorough. The agency had unintentionally captured Breamer in a raid in Dublin, which is how Gamble lost his primary negotiator. Credit was due the CIA, they had interrogated Breamer and provided him a complete composite background packet which included comprehensive details about the arrangements previously negotiated with the Prince. Now, it would be Carmichael's job to get Prince Al-Saud to a pre-arranged location where they could make personal introductions and the final details of the transaction would be recorded. Once the agency had the necessary confirmation of the weapons transfer, the prince would be intercepted. The cash paid to Vinnie would allow the Treasury and financial assets to follow the money. By following the money trail, the agencies would identify Vinnie's financial involvements in other crimes.

After memorizing the exchange details, Jefferies phoned the prince using the number provided by Vinnie. The man answering the phone, said to hold, and relayed the name and intent. Adam retraced the details of the operation, to confirm his intent and identity when the new voice came on the phone. Only then did Prince Al Saud take the call. He expressed great concern about a contact change at this stage of the arrangement and was reluctant to work with someone new, especially after Breamer just up and disappeared. The agency discovered the prince spoke in intelligible English, with only a mild accent.

Immediately Al Saud refused the offer to meet in Chicago, anywhere in Chicago, under any circumstance. He needed time to investigate his new contact. He confirmed his willingness to make the deal, but absolutely it would be he who would set the terms for any meeting.

The Prince paused for several seconds, a conversation was taking place as his hand covered the phone, and then he said, "Atlanta in three weeks; with the weapons."

There was an immediate agreement to his demand from Adam. Wiegand and Gramm have the date and time details, because the call had been made on a secure phone from the limo.

Adam phoned Joni every day he was away, true to his word. It is now that Joni realizes how much she misses him, his physical presence, his smile, his scent. He has become a part of her daily routine. His absence is most noticeable as she stands at the sink eating dinner alone. Dinner has become so unpleasant that she has resorted to eating a bowl of cereal standing in the kitchen, just to get the meal over with. Just like she cannot sleep under the covers on the bed, now there is no lingering over evening meals.

Another momentous change for Joni personally since meeting and spending time with Adam, is that she has developed some new feminine behaviors and 'girly feelings.' These new sensations were reaching the surface of her conscious. Suddenly there is concern about her physical appearance. Her personal hygiene routine now included wearing Beautiful perfume daily since Adam had commented on how nice it smells. Because of the desire to look presentable at all times, she decided to treat herself to a massage, facial, pedicure and manicure while Adam was away. She spent the day at a spa, but enjoyed the results of smooth skin, shapely eyebrows, smooth heels, leaving her feeling more confident in her appearance. Never a shopper, Joni found herself at the mall looking for some new undergarments and something more attractive and appealing than her normal t-shirt nightgowns.

Adam was once again on a plane, but this time headed home to his Joni. Usually his time was spent recalling or memorizing the details of a meet, but Joni finds a way to creep into his thoughts. Today, it is the tea the flight attendant brings him. Oh no, it tastes nothing like the lemonade tea Joni made, but that glass of tea carries his mind to their first day together. Sitting in that plane, miles above the ground, he can still smell her perfume and visualize her smile. He catches himself grinning like a teenager with an erection beginning to form. Shit, so much for memorizing the details he decides.

As much as Adam hates to admit it, Wiegand is correct on one aspect about his relationship with Joni. She is a total distraction for him, in fact an obsession would be a better description. Being with her means protecting her too. The dual focus means his jobs do not get the full attention needed always. This makes Adam a danger to himself and to those working on the case around him. It is why he is committed to seeing this mission through, but leaving the agency by the end of the year. All aspects of his future might be in limbo, but he wants a genuine chance at a normal life with her.

As he sits on the plane, it occurs to him that he has fallen deeply in love with the most amazing woman he has ever met. Actually, he knows that he has loved her since the first day in the garden. Divine intervention. It is must be why he stopped all those years ago. The compassionate act of helping her has kept him barely human these past years. Remembering her agony and pain, the memories of her physical suffering, played on his mind that he is not the man that he has pretended to be for so many years. The legend that is Adam Carmichael had almost swallowed him up…taken over Tony Jefferies' life, until he found himself in her company again.

Adam had changed his flight to get home a day early. So, she isn't expecting him until tomorrow. He is so anxious to see her he goes directly to her house when he lands. Bandit was laying by the door when he came in, so he stopped to pet him and greet him too, because for the first time in his life, he had missed a dog.

She is standing in the kitchen, her favorite place to be, looking at him with wide surprised eyes. Adam went to her and turned her to hold her close. "You smell wonderful. I couldn't stay away from you any longer. I never want to leave home again." Adam murmured in her ear as he held her. The word home had taken on a new meaning for each of them. He didn't mean the house, but home was within each other's arms.

Joni stroked his face, feeling the bits of stubble on his cheeks. He had not shaved today, leaving his skin feeling rough when he nuzzled on her neck. The new texture against her skin was very exciting, sending quivers down her spine, and making her nipples hard.

"Do you like this look?" He questioned. He was rubbing his hand along his jaw line, causing a sandpaper sound as he stroked back and forth, while noticing the physical response of Joni's body.

"I like you any way I can get you, Mr. Carmichael. I'm so surprised to see you tonight, but I'm so glad you are here." They clung to each other, their bodies melding into each other. The fire that was desire was quickly becoming lust as they stood in that embrace. The kisses became deep, then Adam was nibbling on her bottom lip, all while he rubbed his hands up and down her waist. Then he grabbed Joni's butt, pulling her hips even closer to his body.

"This is how much I missed you." His erection pushed against her thigh as he held her in place. Their lips were locked, tongues exploring deep and lingering as each moaned as their hands were exploring each other.

"Oh, Adam, I have missed you so." Joni whispered as she feathered kisses on his neck.

Except her exact words were, "Oh, Jake, I have missed you so."

Adam's heart seized at hearing that name. He released his hold on her and planted butterfly kisses on her eyelids and replied, "Honey, I have missed you too. How can I help with dinner?" He stepped around her to see what was on the stove.

When Adam looked around the kitchen he found she had shopped for all of his favorite foods, including his favorite wine. The lettuce they planted had been picked, ready to become the base of a salad. Pork chops were marinating in the fridge and a couple of bottles of chilled wine, her menu for lunch tomorrow.

The sudden change of ambiance was unpredicted, but Joni thought after her crazy episode days before he left, he was right to go slow. It was obvious he wants to be here. There is no confusing his physical response being near her.

They reveled at sharing a dinner together and to celebrate they drank an entire bottle of wine. After washing dishes, they settled onto their usual places on the couch. Joni snuggled up against him, her head resting on his chest and his arm draped over her shoulders. The final glasses of wine sets on the coffee table in front of them. Adam shifts slightly, grasping her shoulder, drawing her nearer. His gaze is quite intent when he questioned her. "Joni, do you want to be with me? I mean do you think of me when we are apart?"

The head nodding began immediately. "I'm not sure why you are asking. I'm almost embarrassed to tell you, but you are the only thing I think about every moment of every day. If you changed your mind and ended this relationship, I'm not sure I could live through the heartache. Since you have come into my life, I am alive again. You have breathed life into the empty shell of a body that used to be me. Inside, my heart was hurt so badly. When I think about my past it still does. Adam, you are my new beginning and I can imagine you as my end, which is scary because sometimes I'm afraid we are moving too fast and other times we are not going fast enough. We still have so much to learn about each other…"

He cut off the declaration with wet, soft lips caressing her neck. "I just need to know you aren't playing the field and planning to break my heart." Gently he stroked her cheek and pushed a piece of hair out of her face.

"Ha ha ha" Joni chuckled. "Like I have so many options…so many guys beating down my door. I have only opened my door to you and even then, I had to force you in here with my shotgun." She teased him.

She took his hand and intertwined their fingers. Joni trusts Adam completely and does not want to lose him. But her own self-doubts might jeopardize this relationship. She decided this might be a safe time to have an awkward discussion.

"Adam, I need to tell you I'm very scared about having sex with you." Her head was nodding back and forth again.

He looked at her with his eyebrows in a V, disturbed as to this statement.

"Oh, don't get me wrong. I enjoyed sex before and can't wait to experience it with you. But remember our discussion about being Catholic? Well, I think some of those old fashion notions are stuck in my head. When I open my legs and invite you in, I am letting you very close to my heart. It is not sex for me, but lovemaking. I think I told you this before. We will need to be in love before I can let you near my heart. Do you understand? Can you be patient with me?" She pleaded with him to understand.

"Yes ma'am. Reading you loud and clear." He thought he understood.

After this night, Joni and Adam became constant companions, but they still have not slept together. They've been on the verge many times, but Jake makes a sudden appearance, interrupting the mood. Adam readily admitted that most men would throw in the towel regarding a relationship at this point. Oddly, the wait makes him want her more, but her calling him Jake throws off his equilibrium. She admitted that she is afraid. Afraid that Adam will leave her; afraid that her heart will be broken beyond repair. It is a reasonable fear for someone who has lost so much. Only time will convince her that he is here to stay.

16.

Joni often jokingly reminds Adam their first day together began when she brought him into her home at the end of a shotgun. So, on this day while Adam was cleaning his gun, he suggested that she do the same. When Joni told him that she had never cleaned her gun, Adam almost choked. Boy those were the wrong words to say to a man who carries a gun for a living. He scolded her because she had no idea how dangerous a dirty gun could be, but it had him thinking that she might not know how to do anything more than threaten the use of force with the gun. Adam lectured her on the importance of being ready to use a weapon if you draw it.

Now that Joni had confessed how ill-equipped she was to handle a gun, he made plans to remedy the situation. Guns were an area of expertise for him and as a gun owner, he insisted that she should also be proficient with her weapons. Adam offered to take her to a firing range and she apprehensively accepted.

Joni told him that she had been scared to be home alone so she bought a gun, but had put it in the closet, without ever taking it out of the case. She did in fact have a 9MM, but had never fired it, nor had it ever been cleaned. Believing that just having it in her hand would be enough to scare someone.

He called the Marksman Firing range and booked a booth for that very afternoon. They gathered all their weapons and left for the range. Adam didn't want the training to be daunting for her, so he did not rush through any portion of the process. First, they viewed the safety video about how to handle the weapon while in the building. Next, they toured the firing area and he showed her how to place the targets on the trolley. He instructed her on how to check for properly fit the eye protectors and handed her ear plugs before they went into the booth for actual target practice.

In her previous life, Joni would be intimidated and self-conscious of making mistakes when learning something so fundamentally new. She commented Adam was a great instructor, but he said it was because she listened and took instructions well. Adam was impressed that it only took a little guidance to get her to hold her weapons correctly, site in, and learn to squeeze rather than pull a trigger.

He let her hold his Smith and Wesson 1911 and shared that it is a 45-caliber handgun. Joni said she liked how it looks. His gun has a satin finish on stainless steel with matte black safety, magazine release button, and slide release leaver for contrasting features. The wooden grip panels have a fish scale pattern, giving his weapon a very distinctive look she thought. Adam tried to teach her by example. He fired first, unloading three magazines, and hitting the target at center mass with every shot. He shares that he has been firing weapons for more than twenty years, which makes the process look easy.

Nervously she accepted the challenge, but did not let his experience intimidate her. He encouraged her, but required her to practice, emptying several magazines into the target, until she could hit the center mass consistently. She was very pleased with herself the first time she hit the target. Adam and everyone else in the facility thought she would jump the moon when she hit the bulls-eye the first time.

When he handed her a magazine to refill with bullets, she just looked at it. That is when Adam realized she was serious about not understanding her weapons. Joni didn't know how to reload. Patiently, he showed her how to properly feed the bullets into the magazine. Strength was lacking in her fingers, plus the spring was tight, but both problems will change with time and practice he assured her.

Joni was thankful that all the work with her 9MM made her a better shot with the shotgun. They only practiced one day with the shotgun and she was rewarded with a high five from Adam after just two hours of training. Her shoulder was bruised and sore, but it felt great knowing she could impress Adam with her new-found ability. What he did say is they would continue to target practice…often. After three long days at the range, she was damn good with both weapons. The ultimate compliment came when Adam commented he would trust her covering his back.

After training so hard with her guns, Adam thought Joni might be surprised to learn that weapons can be used for fun too. He decided to take her to a turkey shoot.

Joni rode over in the truck in complete silence, listening to Adam sing to his new Florida Georgia Line CD.

She was trying to fathom why he thought she wanted to run around a field and shoot a turkey. But she will try it if he thinks this would be something she might like.

Besides, she swore that she was open to trying new things. Then again, she hadn't asked for an explanation or details, and he hadn't volunteer any information.

When they arrived at their destination in Suffolk, they found about forty cars and trucks parked around the unplanted peanut field. He took her hand and began the explanation. He pointed out the ten bales of hay. Targets were pinned to the hay, indicating ten stations are set up, so that ten people can shoot each round. Everyone gets three shots at the target. The person with the three best shots, meaning the closest to the bull's eye, wins the prize for that round. Tonight, the prizes are hams, frozen turkeys, and a full pork loin. Usually, the prize is a frozen turkey, hence the name, turkey shoot. It costs $5 per person, per round.

The sponsors provide the shotgun slugs, so that everyone is shooting the same type of ammo, but you bring your own weapon.

Joni laughed and shared she envisioned running around chasing a turkey while Adam signed them up and paid for all ten rounds. She swatted his backside when he said he thought so based on the expression on her face during the drive over.

Marie had made a thermos of hot chocolate for the night. Adam just about choked on his chocolate when Joni asked why they weren't drinking a beer. He reprimanded her for even thinking about mixing firearms and alcohol. Then he swiftly reminded her about the safety talk they had while practicing at the firing range. "Remember, weapons and alcohol don't mix well." Adam also advised her to stay close, because they will want to avoid the idiots that are not heeding that very lesson.

Ms. Crawford was anxious, but managed to hit the target in all rounds. Adam stood behind her, whispering for her to breathe and squeeze the trigger. Joni did much better with just three days practice than Adam expected. He was very generous with his praise, knowing she wasn't going to earn a prize, but showing she had been in contention in a couple of rounds.

Adam on the other hand, an expert marksman, cannot let on, nor can he win as often as he should. Joni was very proud of her instructor; she was beaming as they strolled over to the check in booth to collect a turkey and a ham he had allowed himself win.

Because he is spending so much time with Joni, Adam often doesn't make it to the gym during the week. Being fit and strong is crucial for his personal persona and his overall safety, as well as being able to keep her safe. So shortly after their fire arms lessons, Adam surprised Joni once again. But this time by bringing her some hot pink

Brook's running shoes. He knew it was a gamble, that she might be insulted, but he explained his need to exercise. Mr. Carmichael talked about running rather than just walking Bandit. As she got faster, they could start taking a run right after work, with or without Bandit.

Honestly, the guns had scared Joni less than this one pair of shoes. Short of PE in school, Joni had never run on purpose. But she instantly realized this is something Adam wanted and probably needed to do. She knew this would be difficult and painful, but once again she accepted his offer.

In many ways, Joni has some natural athletic abilities. Adam made it fun because he loved to chase her around the park. She would laugh and smile as she was running from him. The deal was if he caught her, he could throw her over his shoulder and carry her around like a trophy. At first Adam caught her easily, but in just a couple of weeks, she got better at running in a zigzag move to avoid him, as well as getting quicker. Joni alleged she hated being carried around, but sometimes she did let Adam catch her.

It only took about ten days before she could jog three miles, keeping a close pace with Adam. Now he added yet another program to their daily exercise routine. Some hand to hand combat techniques and skills. Joni forgot to tell him about her fear of the shoes but did now. This additional training makes her worry about what is really outside her front door. She explained that ignorance is bliss. He clarified everyone is at risk and since he can't be with her to protect her every minute he wants to train her about how to protect herself.

Again, he was great at explaining the techniques, when to use them and then being patient while she practiced them on him. When Joni had a puzzled look with a "frowny" face, he realized it was too much information too quick. He broke down that specific maneuver into bite size pieces that she could process. Nothing about the movements felt normal and none were natural feeling for Joni, fueling her feelings of concern. But she did notice all these techniques seemed second nature to him.

Her instructor often mentioned scale versus skill. That size wouldn't matter if she used her skills properly. Some of the additional tips they talked about were techniques like, s*oft to hard*-slam the palm of your hand forcefully into a nose. *Hard to soft*-jam your foot into a man's crotch. He taught her critical skills, like how to get out of a choke hold and how to pin someone's arms.

Between the running and the daily physical exercise, the change to Joni's body was almost immediate. She acknowledged that she had been on the thin side, mostly because she didn't eat much before meeting Adam.

But her body was flabby. Adam had brought a few hand weights for her to use, so coupled with the running, her body was getting toned and firm. She had even thought to herself that she won't be so embarrassed to take off her clothes when the time finally does arrive!

17.

He was distraught because they were already running late because of Vinnie's earlier calls and his maniacal mood swings. Now they were heading back to his house for the theater tickets he had forgotten. Joni had been inside of his house a couple of times, but only to pick up or drop off things. Unlike most women she had shown little interest in his house, stuff, or income. Adam acknowledged, Joni had made no demands, or offers, to split their time between houses. Of course, there are secrets in this house, so he has never suggested they spend time here either. Surprisingly, neither wondered why. They both subconsciously knew her house as home and the place they were designing a new beginning together.

This night Joni asked if she could use the restroom before they take off again, because she had been rushed out the door because of the required extra stop. He had been ignoring his cell, but his land line phone was ringing and Adam quickly realized his mistake of answering it while he waited for her.

He gestured to get her attention and then pointed at the phone and held up one finger to Joni when she came back into the room. Adam went down a short hallway, then turned into his office and closed the door with a bang. It must be a very important call for him to be upset along with the risk being late for the play Joni thought.

Suddenly curious, she decided to take the opportunity to wander and look around his immaculate home. She was mentally comparing the comforts each place offered. While the style of her home was cottage, she decided this would be described as modern, possibly ultramodern. This house had hardwood floors throughout in a dark mahogany or cherry color. After the floors, the next thing she really noticed is how starkly the house was furnished. No rugs anywhere in sight and everything was shiny. The furniture in his living room was black leather with silver nail head embellishment. There is a black lacquer coffee table with glass and chrome side tables. His dining room set was also black with a high gloss finish. Joni grinned while thinking the chairs appear so slick, she might slide off one if she sat down. The kitchen was small, but had a large island separating the kitchen from the dining room. The countertop was black and beige with flecks of mother of pearl. To continue the high impact, all the appliances were stainless steel. It was a beautiful place but seemed cold and sterile compared to her house. She wondered if Adam wanted to change anything about her house after really looking at how he lives here.

The next thing that stood out to Joni was the lack of anything personal, anywhere visible in the house. There were no photos of anyone, no diplomas, no awards, and no trophies, no plants, nothing that indicated this house belonged to Adam Carmichael. But as Joni was giving this situation some consideration, she realized the same thing could be said for her own house. There are only three small photos in a lone brass picture frame that sat on the bedside table. In the very next instant, it occurred to her that picture might disturb Adam while they are lying in the bed together. She decided to move it out of sight as soon as they arrive back home. Smiling, she thought it might also be time to get a framed picture of them together. Definitely, they have been seeing each other long enough that a "couple picture" would be appropriate.

In the office, away from Joni's earshot, Adam is fuming. It is Vinnie calling again, for the millionth time today. He is still pissed the meeting with the prince has been scheduled so far out. It doesn't matter to Vinnie that it was the prince who set the time and place. He says he wants the money in his hand now.

Now Vinnie wants Carmichael to change the meet for earlier. In fact, he wants to meet tomorrow for God sakes. This exact conversation has taken place between Adam and Vinnie at least five times today. Adam knows it is going to take time to again convince Vinnie to leave the current arrangements in place. But he begins listing his rationale for not calling. First of all, the prince will be suspicious. Second, the prince had made this selection for the meet. Third, it was just over a week away. Better to give him time to check out his new contact and not run the risk of losing the deal all together.

For the agent, he is afraid that a sudden change will affect the CIA's ability to cover the meet. Even if the prince agrees to a change of venue or time, Adam cannot be sure to get a message to Wiegand in time for a detail to get set up at a new location.

When Adam had exhausted his list of explanations, he suggested that they carry the discussion over to the morning, when they are both thinking more clearly. What a mistake to say because now Vinnie starts in about Carmichael's fucking personal life crossing over into his work life. Once again, he reminds Adam that part of his job is to be available at a moment's notice and have nothing that can be used as leverage. Seeing someone seriously affects both requirements. So now Carmichael is going to have to listen to him bitch about her too.

While she was waiting for Adam to finish his phone call, Joni was startled by the opening of front door by an older, yet attractive woman, then walking into the house. The woman carried two bags of groceries. Thankfully the bags prevented Joni from letting her insecurities take over and leap to the conclusion that this was someone Adam was seeing. She remembered he had mentioned having a housekeeper. In fact, she had eaten a few of the meals this woman had prepared for Adam.

She's packed us a couple of picnic baskets too, Joni thought fondly. Marie. Her name is Marie, she remembered. "May I help you?" Joni exclaimed as she jumped up to meet the woman near the door.

"No, no. This is everything. Mr. Carmichael doesn't eat at home too often anymore. In fact, he is not home much either." She said with a definite accent, but her tone was not judgmental.

The comment made Joni blush, but at the same time on top of the world. The housekeeper knew she was the reason for Adam's absence from his life at this house. "You must be Marie. My name is Joni. Please let me help you. Adam brags on your cooking and compares mine to yours often. You are a marvelous cook. I've asked Adam to check with you about swapping some recipes." Joni informed her.

Marie was warm and friendly as she conversed with

Joni. They worked together to unpack the bags. Marie watched Joni carefully while she put things away in the cabinets. They discussed Adam's favorite foods and the spices used to make her food so flavorful. Marie said vanilla ice cream with crushed peanuts was Adam's favorite dessert, which was a surprise to Joni, because she thought it was brownies. Joni thought long and hard and couldn't remember Adam ever eating ice cream, but then, she realized there is never ice cream at our house.

Once Vinnie had run out of reasons to change the meet, bitching about Joni, and finally is convinced to leave everything in place, just as the prince had requested. Adam went back into the living room looking for Joni. He unknowingly had left her alone for more than twenty-five minutes. Adam was troubled when he found her Marie, sitting in the kitchen, discussing recipes.

"What have the two of you been up to?" He smiled as he entered the room, but got no immediate response from either woman.

"Well, Mr. Carmichael. If you don't want us ladies to keep little secrets from you, then you mustn't leave your lady friend alone for so long." Marie snapped back at him, with a grin on her face.

"I'm glad the two of you have gotten along so famously, but I'd better get you out of here if we are going to make the play." Adam could feel his adrenaline flowing with urgency to get Joni out of the house.

Marie commented to him as they were walking out the door, "She's a keeper sir."

True to form Adam opened the door to the truck and held Joni's hand as she stepped up into the truck. Though he clasped her hand as soon as he got settled in the truck, he remained silent, distracted, and maybe even flustered Joni noticed. She tried to make small talk with him by telling him about some of the recipes Marie recommended. She stopped talking knowing he hadn't heard a word she said because he was so deep in thought, so far away from where they were sitting.

After some time, she tried again. "You never told me much about Marie, but she was very kind to me. She obviously cares about you and tries to find ways to make you happy, especially when she is cooking for you."

He shook his head yes in agreement. "She gets paid a lot to make me happy. But you're right, she is very good at what she does." Adam told her. Joni has no way of knowing this statement about Marie was not congruent with hers.

As usual, Joni is fully in tune with Adam. Recognizing his tense body language, foul mood, and distraction since taking the urgent phone call has not changed, she simply says to him, "Let's forget the play. Your mind is elsewhere tonight. You will not enjoy the evening when you want or need to be doing something else."

He turned and looked at her in complete surprise. "What about you honey? You would probably like this play."

She caressed his cheek and returns the gaze. "Well, truthfully Mr. Carmichael, knowing your state of mind, I would be worrying about you worrying. So, I wouldn't be enjoying it either."

He shook his head, not wanting to discuss the situation with her. All he could do is tell her he is grateful that she understands. In silence, he drove her home. Adam planted several kisses on her hands before letting her out of the truck.

She stood in front of this man that had brought her nothing but comfort and begged, "Can I help in any way Adam?"

He shakes his head no once again because there is nothing she can do. She is part of his problems.

When Joni was inside the house and Adam had pulled away from the curb, it took just moments to realize how little she knew about Adam's work. What kinds of public relation things would cause him this much stress, especially for him to be so distant and distracted? Very early on there was an unspoken agreement that they would not discuss work at home, which they adhered to still today. Adam had met some of Joni's co-workers when he came into the library and again at the night club. But the only person Joni had met from his work was the illustrious Mr. Sullivan from the Luke Bryan concert!

This was the first time since they started seeing each other that the real world had intruded on their private time. Joni did not like how the world was treating Adam tonight. This problem, well, it was out of her control to help make it better for him, which upset her.

Thank goodness, she suggested they cancel, Adam thought, because Vinnie continued the war path all night. He finally relented to call the prince. Shockingly, the man agreed to move up the meet. Two days, not tomorrow. But Adam knows there is no guarantee the deal will be done. Adam must let Joni know that he is leaving because his flight is scheduled for 7a.m. There is no way he can get over to see her and tell her in person. He decided it was best this way anyway. If he took her in his arms and held her close, he might confess his secrets and not get on the plane.

He called her cell phone while she was out delivering papers. He told her was packing his bag as they were speaking. The issue from last night was not something that could be resolved from here, but demanded his personal attention. But he would check in with her as soon as he arrived. There was a sense of urgency in his voice as they said good-bye.

Joni could hear the stress from last night in his voice still this morning. She could tell from his tone he was upset. This issue, whatever it is, must be very important for him to be called away so quickly. She said a quick prayer for him and pleaded with God to somehow reassure her Adam is not rushing off to another family somewhere else! Damn her insecurity, she chastened herself.

The suddenness of this trip made her very curious about his work life. Her mind was filled with questions. Would Adam need to take his gun? It was always present. Omni-present, handy, but out of sight. If he carried a gun while in town, just with her, he must surely travel with one too, she decided. Is that why he exercises so much and practices his hand to hand combat skills? But why? Why

would he need to be so tactically prepared?

All kinds of questions ran through her mind now.

What kind of public relations work requires a gun? Could it

be because of his "eligible" status that he must protect

himself? Do people hate him because of who he works for?

If Gamble is so notorious, maybe his actions and behaviors

affect Adam. Why would such a capable and talented man

like Adam work for a man like Vinnie?

18.

Adam called Joni immediately upon landing, like he promised her. He did not say where he was staying; only that he would be gone a few days. This is a very delicate situation. The negotiations were expected to be fierce and tense, so it was quite likely he would be unavailable during the day time hours. Adam specified he would make a point to reach her by phone each night around 8 pm. Just before he hung up, he told her how desperately he missed her already. Adam asked if she would please pick him up at the airport when he returned. She is the first thing he wanted to see when he got home.

Wiegand was the next contact Adam made. Though risky, the agency needs to be aware of Vinnie's unpredictability as well as the new agenda. There had been no time to make a drop for the courier before leaving

Virginia. Adam slipped across the street from the hotel to a coffee café. He will use this site to email the details and his exact whereabouts.

Thank goodness Brett was sitting at his computer, because Adam got an immediate response to the encrypted email. Wiegand would dispatch a local agent to check out some contacts that might be utilized in the absence of the scheduled team. Jefferies needs to check back in four hours for more details. During those hours, Adam will contact the prince to confirm the time of the meet, because Vinnie says the weapons are already in Atlanta. The deal can be made right now.

The prince did not take his call, but Adam left a message explaining that the merchandise had arrived in port earlier than expected and it was available for immediate delivery. He asked the prince to contact him to get further instructions.

Vinnie has been blowing up his cell phone, demanding information about the meet. Carmichael calmly asked Vinnie if the call had been placed in reverse-if the prince was the one wanting the change, would Vinnie jump onboard, or would he be skeptical? Finally, Adam asked the obvious question. Is the prince being set up? Is that why the weapons were here already? Carmichael expressed everything about this situation seems like they are managing a situation rather than making a deal. Adam demanded an answer since he is the front man, the one most likely to be targeted or eliminated if things go wrong. Vinnie ignored the questions and the demand for an answer.

Wiegand sent back vague info, because he had no word to confirm unusual activity in Atlanta. No intel about the arrival of merchandise had been found on such short notice, but he was still following up on available contacts. After a follow up email, a sketchy plan was laid out. The place and time to meet with Vinnie, without Adam, was suggested. All that needed to be done by Adam was to set up the site, confirm the location with Al-Saud, then let the agency handle the rest.

Vinnie showed up early at Carmichael's hotel later in the evening. He was on the phone with Joni when Vinnie knocked, but opened the door, and strolled in. Joni happily informs Adam that she and Marie have hit it off. She has gone to his house and is learning to cook some of Marie's recipes.

Next, she mentions the closet in his office, "I want you to know as I was looking around your house, I stumbled into the closet off your office."

Vinnie is pacing while he waits for Carmichael to end the call. Adam quickly give Joni his return flight information. She is thrilled to know exactly when he is coming home. Now she can plan a special dinner from one of the new recipes.

Vinnie is standing over him as Adam sat on the couch talking to Joni. "Is that her, the girl? Vinnie sneered when he asked. Vinnie began the tirade again. He repeated his right-hand man is not to have an ongoing relationship. He has permission to screw every girl on the east coast with his blessing, but there can be no attachment of any type. This relationship puts his entire enterprise in jeopardy and must end now.

After ending the call, Adam stood up and faced off with Vinnie. "I've told you before, my love life is none of your damn business. As long as I can make the deals, handle the arrangements, be at your beck and call, and travel at your command, then what I do with my personal time is completely off limits. It is only if I screw up is there any risk and I have never screwed up, now have I?

Besides, you need me right now Vinnie." Adam summarized the relationship between him and his employer.

Vinnie walked away, moving toward the other side of the room. "Where the fuck is this meeting going down. I need to get my shipment together." Vinnie changed the subject. He is still furious that he does not have absolute control over Carmichael. This new development - Adam refusing to follow his orders or yield to his demands.

The information passed via Wiegand regarding the meet is that Carmichael should attempt to send Vinnie in to make the deal on his own. The agency has secured a meet location. The negotiator tells Vinnie they will be meeting in a private hangar on the airport grounds. Adam explains they have garnered access to the facility by renting a plane, under the guise that they will use their own man as the pilot for this charter. At first the pilot was reluctant to make the deal, but like everyone else, when there are enough zero's behind the number, anything can be arranged Adam chuckled while telling Gamble. Carmichael suggested Vinnie go and check out the arrangements on his own since he didn't seem to trust his right-hand man any longer.

Adam gave Vinnie a paper with the hangar number and exact location at the airport. Vinnie walked away as he began dialing his cell phone, heading out the door.

"Any details or additional arrangements you need to let me in on?" Adam probed him.

"NO, I just have to check in with my wife." Vinnie was gone.

Adam knew he was lying. Vinnie doesn't give a rat's ass about his wife. He had never known him to call his wife unless absolutely necessary. He has something planned, something big or bad is going to happen. Adam was certain a double cross was planned. Instinctively he knew he would have to stay out of or ahead of this mess that Vinnie is calling an exchange.

Early the next morning, Vinnie called Carmichael's room and insisted that they travel together to the meet site. Adam made the excuse he was not ready, but Vinnie gave him fifteen minutes to get ready. Now Adam knows something is up and extracting himself from this meeting is improbable. He has not heard back from Wiegand, so there will be no support backing him up.

A limo drove them to the airport and then to the west side of the grounds, where the private planes were housed. Planning for potential problems, Adam noted there is a fence around this area, preventing private travelers from mingling with public travelers, but it does not offer a checkpoint to prevent entry. When they arrived at the specified hangar, Vinnie insisted they complete an extensive examination of the building inside and out. They combed through every piece of equipment in the place.

Every nook and cranny was explored. Although he is grateful they find nothing out of place, Carmichael realizes the weapons are nowhere to be found either. He chooses to say nothing to Vinnie about his observation.

The appointment with the prince is a couple of hours away. Vinnie and Adam had been present in the hangar for about ninety minutes, searching for anything out of the ordinary, when without warning another limo with a panel truck following closely behind, sped into the open doors of the hangar. The vehicles arrived simultaneously, blocking the only exit to the building.

Vinnie and Adam stopped in their tracks, taken by surprise by the sudden chaos and arrival of the vehicles. They were caught standing in the middle of the room, near the plane. Ten behemoth men dressed in military brown/tan camouflage uniforms and each armed with an AK-47, deftly jumped out of the back of the panel truck, forming a circle around the two men. The ambushed pair wisely and slowly raised their hands above their heads. The newly arrived limo door opened once the armed men had positioned themselves around the two.

Seeing the potentially hazardous situation was under control, the prince gracefully stepped out from behind the protection of his vehicle to confront the men. Adam noticed this man is young, maybe in his latetwenties, certainly as tall as himself, probably 6' 5" inches, and he was wearing a very expensive dark gray suit. Although he looks Middle Eastern, today his English is perfect when he speaks.

Adam hopes to impress upon the prince they will be cooperative, so he speaks first as he slowly lowers his hand to offer a handshake. Carmichael introduces himself and then Vinnie. As he turns to introduce his boss and stakeholder of the weapons, Adam notices the squinting eyes of Vinnie Gamble. A clear indicator he is thoroughly pissed. Thankfully today, Vinnie is coherent enough to remain silent.

Prince Al-Saud faces Gamble and questioned why the insistent demands to exchange weapons today. Was he truly ready to make the exchange, here and now? Vinnie could only say the shipment had not yet arrived at this location, but was in transit. Besides, the prince was early for the scheduled appointment. Prince Al-Saud reminded Vinnie, it was at his insistence and assurance the weapons were ready to be transferred, that this meeting was rescheduled. With a twinkle in his eyes, he revealed he had seen a van full of men being detained at the gate.

The prince calmly clarified with Vinnie that because of this unfortunate delay, he had forfeited the right to choose the exchange details or make any changes to the future plan. Now he will once again select the timetable and place for their next encounter. Exhausting hours of planning and surveillance had gone into his original plan for the weapons exchange and he would not tolerate another change. He pointed at Vinnie, said he would call with details, and then turned on his heels. The prince walked back to his car, slid inside as the armed men reboarded the truck. The two vehicles made their exit from the scene just as swiftly as they came. Two men watched in disappointment as the vehicles drove off.

When Adam looked over at Vinnie, his face was beet red and screwed up in livid anger. "Where the fuck are my guns?" he screamed as he was dialing his cell phone. Before he could finish punching in the number, a blue van pulled into the hangar almost precisely were the prince had been parked moments ago.

"What the hell happened at the gate? Where the fuck have you been?" A ballistic Vinnie reached in, pulled the driver of the van by the collar of his shirt, dragging him through the window, completely out of the vehicle.

"Security stopped us. We got the truck with the guns out of line before they inspected it, but this van was held for a random vehicle check. They let us through after they ran the metal detectors and drug dogs through. Then they looked at the registration. Once they were satisfied, I was allowed through without a further glance." The trembling driver was Eddie. The same Eddie from the boat. He glanced at Carmichael, but turned away quickly.

"Come on Vinnie. No harm, no foul, here. The deal WILL go down, just not on YOUR terms. You heard that for yourself. The prince is interested in your merchandise and is planning to make the trade. He is just not happy with the delivery point today. Let's go home and wait to hear from him." Carmichael suggested as he stepped around Eddie, shifting Vinnie's focus. Eddie shot a look of thanks in Adam's direction.

After throwing a raging tantrum about the missed chance to make the deal, Vinnie unexpectedly decided to

259

stay in Atlanta for a couple of days. Some story about needing to survey his assets and do some damage control.

Adam threw his hand up in the air and flat out announced he was going home. Of course, this declaration caused Vinnie to launch into a new rant about being pussy whipped. Adam didn't care and didn't listen to anything being said. He needed to get away from Vinnie and to check in. Mostly to thank Wiegand for a job well done.

Before heading to the airport, Jefferies slipped back to the coffee shop and signed onto the encrypted system. There was a message in his inbox from Wiegand. Agency could not put a secure plan or rally a support team together quickly enough for this meet to happen. Jefferies was ordered to terminate any direct contact with prince.

Adam emailed Wiegand that he had been unable to extract himself from the mission and the meet had been a go. He details the events pre-and post-arrival of the vehicles and the fact the prince himself had shown. The agent finalized his dispatch with the disclosure that the weapons exchange did not happen. Gamble was now awaiting further instructions from the prince. Carefully signing out and ordering a coffee to keep his cover, Adam practically ran back to the hotel. He needed to let Joni know about his flight change and to pack.

Back in Hampton, while Adam was away, Joni realized he had not yet brought any of the recipes she and Marie had discussed the night of the missed play. With time on her hands, she took a chance and called to ask if Marie was still willing to exchange some recipes. The housekeeper tisk, tisked Mr. Carmichael for not collecting the index cards from the counter. Then Marie suggested they get together this evening soon to prepare a meal and maybe jointly cook some of Mr. Carmichael's favorite dishes. Joni happily accepted the offer. It beat being home alone and spending time with good company would make at least one evening pass quicker.

When Joni opened the door to Adam's house, the aroma of spices, garlic, and tomatoes flooded her senses. Marie shares there is lasagna on the menu for tonight and handed a glass of wine to Joni as she walked into the kitchen. After checking the food in the oven, Marie suggested they take their drinks to the patio to relax for a bit.

Joni was stunned to see the incredible view! The entire back wall of the house was ceiling to floor windows, which astounded her that she had missed this view in her previous visits. Then Joni noticed that there were blinds pulled to the side of the windows. Marie indicated he usually keeps them closed, blocking the magnificent view. She thought if this was her house, she would never pull the blinds, but would take in the spectacular sunset every night from right here.

Adam's house backed up to an inlet which was fed from the Chesapeake Bay. When they stepped onto the patio, there was a cool breeze coming off the water, bringing with it a salty sea water smell and the occasional clang of a bell from a channel buoy. The patio was brick, in a half-moon shape, that extended the length of the house. Upon further observations, she found directly behind the house, a boat launch with a jet ski and a full-size pecan tree growing along the edge of the water with a tire swing hanging from the branches.

Marie was very open about her admiration for Mr. Carmichael. He was a good and fair boss. She shared that in addition to her wages, he had paid her way back to Mexico to visit her family last Christmas, something she could not afford to do on her own.

Adam was always working until lately, she said as she pointed at Joni. Joni must have had a look of shock on her face with this revelation. After finishing their drinks, Marie patted her hand and led her into Adam's office. She closed the door to the room then opened a closet that was hidden when the first door is open. This storage unit was specifically designed for the weapons housed there. The shelves included places for scopes, gripes, and magazines. What captured Joni's attention was every slot was full. Nothing missing. Maybe this trip did not involve a gun after all, she thought feeling some relief.

"Mr. Carmichael must do very dangerous work to need all of these." Marie alleged. "I think you should know about this room. He obviously cares for you very much."

She already knew about his gun and now she is aware of his many guns. This new information causes her some consternation. Why is he teaching her how to use them and how to protect herself when she cannot be with him? Anytime she is with Adam, she knows she is safe, gun or no gun. Men that know him, fear him, she was thinking back to the horrible confrontation and his threat to Sullivan.

When Adam called that night, she told him about having dinner with Marie earlier. Joni confessed to him. "I want you to know as I was looking around your house, I stumbled into the closet in your office."

Adam said nothing to indicate he had heard her comment about the secret closet, so she let it go. Maybe he was upset and didn't know how to reply to her rummaging around his house. He only joked about how much he paid Marie to entertain his girl and was glad she had gotten a good meal out of the visit.

Before they hung up, he gave Joni his return flight information. Her heart soared at the thought of Adam coming home to her. Joni noticed the stress in his voice previously so intense was lessened, but she could hear a hint of tension still lingering. He still did not volunteer his whereabouts or update her about the problem that had carried him away. Gleefully, Joni told him she would fix a special dinner since he was so anxious to be home again. It was then she realized a piece of her life was missing because he was absent.

19.

The next morning Joni showered as soon as she got back from the paper route. She wanted to be at the airport early. Adam had given her his updated flight information and was now due in at 9:17 a.m. She wanted everything to be perfect when he got home. The house was clean, laundry hanging on the clotheslines and windows open to let in the fresh air. The yard work was also complete. There was nothing to distract them from enjoying their time together.

As Joni dressed, she thought about the budding relationship and how memories of Jake seemed to be receding. Part of her believed it was good that Jake was becoming a part of the past. That new memories were being made and she was no longer trying to live in the past. But it seemed her heart pushed Jake to the forefront of her thoughts, making it difficult to step completely out of their history.

Finding a parking spot at the airport was easy because she had arrived about forty minutes early. Talk about anxious for his return! Joni doubled checked the arrival board. He was coming in from Atlanta she learned per the information board and his flight was listed as arriving on time. With nothing else to do, she ducked into the coffee shop to wait.

The coffee was some of the worst she had ever drank. Boy was she wrong. No amount of sugar and cream could make that cup better. It was old and bitter, but provided the opportunity to do something while her thoughts drifted back to Adam Carmichael.

She started the journey down memory lane when she recalled their first coffee date. How far they had come from that night, but what does she want to happen with this relationship? She acknowledges they are friends for sure, but they aren't just experiencing friendly feelings for each other. The electricity between them can be felt each time they touch. And then there's that way her heart and breathing race when she is around him. Then insecurity joins her doubts making her question to what is she really entitled.

Her mind snapped back to reality when the loudspeaker announced the arrival of his flight. Quickly she made her way to the restroom for a quick potty break and to check her appearance before meeting Adam. Of course, there is a line a mile long to use the stalls, but she must wait all because of that one terrible cup of coffee.

After making the final check in the mirror, she must rush to the terminal waiting area. Joni was caught up in her own thoughts of how she wanted to start her conversation with Adam when she rounded the corner to the passenger arrival area. From her left, she heard a female voice shout "Adam". She turned looking for the owner of that voice. A long leggy, beautiful, young blonde woman ran and jumped into Adam's arms while wrapping those forever long legs around his waist. Joni froze in place; her feet wouldn't move and she couldn't break her stare. Thankfully, the couple couldn't see her from her vantage point at the corner of the hallway.

Suddenly, the spasms cramping logical thinking relaxed a little, allowing her feet to mobilize. There was just enough thought to release her, allowing her to run out of the airport. Joni felt sick to her stomach. Feelings of betrayal, embarrassment, foolishness, and anger, all attacked her at the same time. Her mind was exploding with shock and disbelief. Was this really the same man she was just contemplating a potential future? Tears were streaming down her cheeks, although she couldn't remember when she had started crying.

By the time Joni reached the car, the coffee flavored bile had risen into her throat and there was nothing she could do to stop it. The vomit erupted. She stood right next to the car and let her stomach empty its contents onto the parking lot. Mentally she was screaming at herself for being so stupid. Now she was embarrassed that she couldn't stop the physical reaction to her pain.

Her thoughts become a tirade. 'He must have forgotten to tell his other girlfriend he asked me to pick him up. Or did he forget and ask me too? Well, Joni, neither of you ever said this was an 'exclusive' relationship. Just because you let yourself believe that, doesn't mean it was so. Maybe if you would have slept with him, it would have been exclusive! Maybe she is just his booty call. Oh, my God, how stupid are you? If he had that young blonde thing as a booty call, why on earth would he be wasting time with you? He is very eligible and handsome, you've thought that all along. It was just craziness that let your mind run away with you! He never said he loved you. In fact, he's never actually tried to bed you. But he has implied it is what he wants to do. You must be a sympathy case for him. How could you have been so blind to what was so very obvious today? You let yourself imagine this was a relationship.'

All of these thoughts were racing through her mind. Each thought connecting with the next like a train barreling down a track with no brakes. The sight of the young woman with the man she had just imagined as her future were now branded in her brain.

Back inside, Claire had been running down the terminal hallway, announcing her presence at the airport by screaming Adam's name at the top of her lungs. Adam turned just in time to see her coming at him. Claire jumped into his arms and wrapped her legs around him as she hugs him around the neck. Quickly, he placed her feet back on the ground and tells her that behavior is inappropriate now that she is an adult. Especially unfitting for a young woman with a fiancée.

She tells him she is just so excited about running into him because he hasn't been around for a while. Claire tells Adam she is just back from her trip to Boston, where she finally got to meet her future in-laws. Adam is inattentive to the conversation, so he informs Claire that someone is meeting him as he looks all around for Joni.

The more Adam searches for Joni, the more curious Claire becomes about the woman. She follows him through the airport and announces that in all the years she has known Uncle Adam, he has never had a woman meet him at the airport. In fact, she isn't sure she had ever seen Uncle Adam seek out a woman. Completely out of character she advised him.

Although he tried numerous times, Joni is not answering her cell or home phone. After waiting twenty minutes longer, Claire politely offers to give him a ride

home. Carmichael honestly just wants to take a taxi to

Joni's, but Claire is Vinnie's daughter. He doesn't want

Claire to inadvertently relay to Vinnie how concerned

Adam was about his woman's failure to appear. Uncle

Adam tells Claire, his flight plans had changed so maybe

Joni got the times mixed up. Claire is unmerciful and

relentless in her teasing - going on and on about the

figment of his imagination, a woman he calls Joni.

Somehow Joni managed to make her way home,

although she doesn't remember driving. The car was

driven straight into the garage where she pulled down the

door and runs into the house. Inside she bolted the back

door to keep the world outside. The house phone was

ringing. When she picked it up, the caller ID showed it was

Adam's cellphone. No way. There is no way could she

speak to him this upset. She will have to calm herself and

stop crying before talking to him. She can't let him know

how much it hurts; that she had become attached to him. As soon as the land line stopped ringing her cell phone began and it is him. Joni unplugged the home phone line and turned off her cell.

The image of Adam with the beautiful, young blonde was like a video on replay in her mind. The scene was viewed at least a hundred times and she cursed herself through each frame for not seeing the possibility that Adam could be seeing someone else. Her thoughts raged against herself – the words stupid, old woman, chanted over and over. These words became a self-deprecating mantra, the narrative she heard each time she replayed the mental video from the airport.

Once Claire dropped Adam off at his own house, he immediately called the library and checked her schedule. Joni was not working today, Lydia informed him sweetly.

'Ok, so where is she?' His mind drifts to all the worst possible scenarios. He began praying she has not had an episode, a breakdown. Shit! What if she's remembered?

He jumped in his truck and went directly to her house. Her car is in the garage and Bandit is not barking, all indicators that she is home. The back door is locked, not typical for her. Most of the windows are closed, but a few on the back of the house are open. She is not moving about. He decided to drive down Chesapeake Ave, just in case she is out, walking Bandit.

Joni was not walking and nowhere around the park either. Adam got back in his truck and turned it around headed back to his house, not sure what he should do next. The real suspicion is that she is avoiding him, but why is the question he can't immediately answer.

Maybe she needs her space this time, he decided. Whatever THIS is, it kept her from coming to the airport, he thought. 'THIS is going to be bad.' There is no way Adam can truly rest without knowing what has happened. After pacing around his house, he decided he needs to be at their house. Once again, he finds himself in his truck traveling across town. When he arrives, he uses the key she gave him for the back door. Bandit greeted him just like always, but not Joni.

Exhaustion had finally taken over when she fell into her bed. Which is where he found her, sound asleep. Maybe she was sick, a thought that had not crossed his mind until now. Adam checked and found her cell was turned off and her home phone was unplugged. This makes perfect sense he muses. He felt better knowing she was just ill. He would let her sleep if she felt so bad that it kept her from coming to the airport. He would come back later and check on her. Adam walked out of the house feeling relieved.

When Adam closed the back door, Bandit jumped onto the bed with Joni, which woke her. In an instant, she remembered why she had been crying, the tears started flowing again. The hate mantra started over, triggering gut wrenching sobs.

Once again, sleep prevailed, although her body continued to hiccup in her sleep. The house was dark and night had fallen outside when Joni finally woke up. She got out of the bed only for Bandit's need to go outside. While he was in the yard, she turned on the alarm clock which was set for 3:45 am. Joni brought the dog back inside, shut a couple of windows, closed the blinds, changed into a nightgown, and went to the bathroom before plopping back onto the bed.

All the nagging doubts that had plagued her in this relationship reared up like Godzilla and began stomping over all the rational thoughts of what she knows to be true.

She imagined Adam enjoying her company only because of their similar age and the many shared common interests and experiences. They were able to discuss history, politics, religion, art, music or any of a variety of subjects. Maybe he had changed his mind about wanting children. It would make sense he would want someone to take care of him as he grows older and have heirs to carry on his name. Joni's thoughts and heart were trying to find a rational excuse for what her eyes had witnessed.

She eventually found solace in sleep, resting for a few hours. The jangle of the alarm startled her awake. The clanging sound revived the memory of what she witnessed at the airport. Joni was crying before she crawled out of the bed.

The last paper had been delivered and somehow, she had made her way back home. Though she had passed the entire route, it had been done on autopilot. Her mind continued to replay the events of yesterday along with all the negative narrative she could conjure up about herself. Hopefully, no one would try to call about a missed paper, because she knew she was not going to plug the phone in or turning the cell back on yet. Still not ready, not strong enough to face him, she stashed the car back in the garage. She let Bandit out for his morning exercise, dumped some food in his bowl and anxiously waits for him to finish his business. She knew only one way to survive heartache. That meant resurrecting the old routine.

"Come on old girl, you didn't play the game well enough...you lost. YOU are meant to be alone, stupid." She repeated to herself. Thank goodness for autopilot, because the routines were naturally coming back. "Ok, let's get started on laundry. Empty the basket on the floor, sort lights and darks into different piles. Fill up the soap, fabric softener and start the washer." See you can do this, she instructed her body. She decided to start with chores that never included Adam. Joni swept the kitchen floor and cleaned the bathroom, all while tears escaped her eyes. Autopilot was not completely effective today, because all the chores were performed while crying. It only took a couple of hours to complete all the duties she could think of doing.

Adam had eventually fallen asleep, after hours of listening to Vinnie rants on the phone. But unfortunately, sleep overtook him before remembering to set the alarm. It was 6:30 when he woke. He was unaware of how the stress of yesterday had made him so tired. 3:45 had come and gone. He had slept when he should have been helping Joni. Hopefully, she is still asleep and they can just deliver papers late, he thought.

There was still no answer at either door, but he can hear the dryer running, which means she has been up. It is possible she has taken Bandit for a walk, because he isn't barking again today. He called to her just to be sure she wasn't asleep. He contemplated going in the house again, but because of the dryer, he hoped she might be showering, so he waited and called out to her a few more times.

Because of the intimacy of the act she watched Adam share with another woman, for her, their relationship was over. It never occurred to her that Adam would stop by her house. Call maybe. The sound of him pounding on the front door and jiggling the doorknob, trying to get in startled her. He called her name several times, but she did not, no, she could not move. She remained stuck in place at the kitchen sink.

When he left the porch, she peeked out the kitchen window and could see he was sitting in his truck, cellphone in hand. Both her phones were off, but she could guess because of his presence, he was calling her.

He came back up on the porch and tried the door again, shouting her name repeatedly. Adam concluded she must have taken Bandit for a walk. Believing wholeheartedly, she should be home shortly, this time gave him a chance to check in at the office. Staring briefly at the door, the barrier that stood between him and her, he finally got in his truck and left.

Joni's resolve weakened momentarily. She prayed for strength to not call out or run to him. While she watched, she noticed how exquisitely handsome he looked in his navy suit. The suit meant he was dressed for work. Hopefully, once he leaves, he would be gone and out of her life for good she thought. No, not for good, but forever. That thought caused the tears to flow again. She wondered how on earth could there be more tears.

Again, her mind tried to justify his behavior because it had not been a sexual relationship. No commitment. What was his favorite phrase - no harm, no foul? Yup that's it. She decided they had been hanging out as friends, rather than starting a forever relationship, like she had allowed herself to imagine. The intimate kisses and

touching were just friends with a little benefit. That must

be what happened.

20.

Joni's head was throbbing and she was physically aching from all the conflicting thoughts, the anguish of the loss, the anger of being misled, and the tears that continued to plague her. After a long hot shower, she put on her favorite nightgown, took two Tylenol PM's even though it is only 8 am. She reluctantly assumed her place on top of the covers knowing the pillows smelled of him. Joni is depending on the medicine to bring a much-needed escape. What she wanted, no, what she needed from the medication was to turn off her mind. Because now the reality is Adam has left the porch and chosen someone else.

After checking with his secretary and verifying nothing needed his immediate attention at his office, Adam headed back to Joni. This time he parked out by the garage and let himself in the back door.

He was slightly distraught to see Bandit had joined her on the bed which is not typical either. Joni must really be feeling bad for her to let him climb up onto the bed. He shooed Bandit out of the way so he could sit on the edge. His hand touched her forehead, feeling for a temperature. He asked, "You must be feeling terrible to still be in bed at this hour. Let me fix you something to eat, honey. Do you need me to get you some medicine or call the doctor?"

The sound of his voice and the feel of his touch in her dream unnerved her into a sitting position. 'Crap, this is real. He is here and he is touching me. This is not a dream.' Joni began pushing herself backwards on the bed, out of his reach. She could see the look of bewilderment registered on his face. Knowing her eye are glassy from all the tears she has cried and the medication she has taken, he might think she is ill, but she wanted to yell at him. 'Damn you, I'm not sick, just heart broken,' but the words didn't form.

He was staring at her with a questioning look on his face, shocked by her erratic behavior and now concerned about the severity of her illness. "I've been incredibly worried since you weren't at the airport yesterday. At first, I thought maybe you couldn't get off work, then couldn't reach me because my cell was turned off. When I couldn't get you on your phone, I just knew you needed me here. Please tell me you didn't pass papers feeling so under the weather."

He continued to look at her as she pushed herself up against the head board, still trying to put more distance between them. Adam was oblivious to the terror and anger she felt. He reached out and started rubbing her foot before she had managed to get it out of his reach. Joni knew her body was going to betray her anger and confusion. She could already feel the desire building, just because he was touching her damn foot. Joni looked at him with wild eyes and snatched her foot out of his clasp and pulled the nightgown over it so it was safely covered. Her hands found the blanket and pulled it up around her neck, to keep any skin from being exposed to his touch again. She was thinking, 'This man is a traitor, but so is my body. It will betray me as well.' She was trying to fortify her position of rejecting him, trying to be strong. Strong enough to let him go.

Suddenly some words were forming, not only in her brain but on her lips. "If I had needed your help, I would have called you. I didn't call you, so don't worry about the papers." She lashed out at him. "In fact, everything here is fine. I didn't need you this morning and I don't need you here now. You feel free to go on about your day." She snapped at him. Her resolve was weakening. He needed to be gone, out of this room and her life, very soon.

He tipped his head to one side, his eyes wide with confusion. "What is wrong with you? You sound mad at me…are you angry at me? Tell me what is going on!" he pleaded.

Joni's entire body leaned forward when she launched back at him. "What is wrong with me? How dare you ask me that? After I have confided my deepest, darkest fears, you ask what is wrong with me?" was tossed back at him. "Adam, I cannot, no I will not be part of a three-person relationship. Although we never said it, I thought we were moving toward a committed relationship, something more than friends. I'm not up to a competition. My heart can't stand to be hurt…not another loss. This rollercoaster ride is stopping here right now!" The words lost some of their emphasis through her tears.

"Joni, I have no idea what you are talking about. You are always the one that brings a third person into our relationship – not me. I compete with the memory of Jake every day! What on earth did I do that has you so upset with me?" he asked with shock in his voice. He was standing and facing her now.

She pushed herself onto her knees, kneeling upright in the center of the bed as she began shouting hysterically at him, "how can you stand there and say that to me? At least Jake is a memory. I saw you at the airport yesterday, with the blonde girl."

"What the hell are you talking about? I did not see anyone else, blonde or otherwise at the airport. Where on earth did you get that idea." he paused as he was thinking about the airport.

Her finger was pointing at him, stabbing in the air as she said, "I SAW YOU at the airport yesterday with that young, blonde girl. The way she jumped into your arms and wrapped her legs around you. She is young, beautiful, spontaneous, you know, everything I cannot be. If that is what you want, why have you been here with me? I let myself believe that…" she couldn't finish because she was crying. The pain of facing him, knowing he was no longer hers. It was almost too much to bear.

Suddenly her arms dropped to her sides. "Adam, I saw you with her at the airport. I saw you with my own eyes. Please don't make me feel more stupid than I already do." Joni whispered, but the disgust in her voice was evident.

"Oh my God. You saw Claire. She did jump on me, but I didn't think of it like you have. She is my boss' daughter, but she thinks of me as her uncle. Honey, she is the one getting married next month. The wedding I told you about." He said smiling, because now everything had been explained away.

"Why would she feel so comfortable jumping into another man's arms out in public like that?" Joni hissed at him, not letting him out of this situation so easily.

"God Joni. I don't know, maybe because she is twenty. Who knows what goes on in a young mind these days? Probably she didn't think anything about it, she just jumped. I pushed her off me and told her it was inappropriate, because she isn't a kid anymore. I let her know she shouldn't be jumping onto Uncle Adam any longer." He was desperately trying to understand. "She waited with me at the airport. Hoping to meet the woman that Uncle Adam was searching for all over the airport. When you didn't show up, she gave me a ride to my house. I've been trying to reach you since I got home."

Reality Check! The stupidity of her snap judgment began to register in Joni's mind. Her eyes widened with surprise and then, what, dismay? The tears welled up again and she is shaking her head frantically NO.

Something is still wrong, Adam realizes they are still not ok.

The embarrassment of such a monumental mistake was powerful. How could she have been so mistrusting of Adam and rushed into such foolish scenarios about what she had seen? Why didn't she just ask him about the situation rather than leaping to wrong conclusions? This is just one more reason this relationship must end. Joni decided she doesn't know how to be in a relationship. If trusting what she feels and honestly knows is so difficult…well, it's just better to end this now.

There was no strength in her body to keep her upright on her knees any longer. Joni dropped down onto the bed. "You need to leave, right now. I can't do this. This is just proof positive that I don't know how to be in a relationship. You deserve better than this…than me. I don't know how…what I am supposed to do…how I am supposed to trust. When what I saw hurt so badly? Please Adam, go. Just leave me alone." She cried as she began pushing herself away from him again. Her head was shaking back and forth, saying no uncontrollably with tears streaming down her face as she tried to escape his gaze.

Adam was just as confused as Joni. Everything he has done and fought for has been for her, to make a life with her. He cannot just let her walk away, to let go of her love over something as stupid as this petty mistake. His instincts took over. Adam reached out and grabbed Joni by the wrists. His strength made easy work of pulling her back toward him. "Oh, no. I am not letting you retreat from this, not from us. I do not accept your decision. Joni, I know you are scared about being hurt. I have done everything within my power to keep that from happening. This relationship is about us, not just you. My feelings are hurt that you didn't trust me enough to ask me about yesterday. That you would run and hide from me. We are not throwing us away because you are embarrassed, do you understand?

Good grief, when do you think I would have time to be with someone else? Did you ask yourself that question? I am here every waking moment of everyday, except for when I am at work. You are what I think of first thing in the morning, last thing at night and most of the time in between. I can't wait to be with you. This is where I want to be…you do not get to throw it away!" He spoke forcefully as he looked her in the eyes. He had pulled Joni up onto her knees, while placing the palms of her hands on his chest, so she could feel his heart beating rapidly.

Next, as he continued to gaze at her and while she continued to cry, he placed her arms around his neck. He used his free hands to reach around her back and pull Joni tightly into his body.

She was mumbling, shaking her head, and tears were still flowing, "No. No I can't do this."

"Oh honey. Yes, you can and yes, we are. I am going to show you how much I love you Joni. You are the only one for me. I know you love me, but are too afraid to show it. We are going to make love right here and right now." His hands pulled the nightgown over her head before she could process what he was saying.

Her body was betraying her with his every touch. Adams lips found hers and her lips were eager to greet his. Her body took control and her hands were caressing his body. All the rest of her body is defying her head nods and responding yes to his touch. But damn, her head is still shaking no.

"I can't yet, I'm not ready," Joni whispered in his ear as his mouth was exploring her body.

"Yes, yes we are. We will do this together like we do everything else. Look at me. I am right here and I am going to stay here with you." Adam had pulled her close, bringing her arms to his chest. He grabbed Joni around her upper back with his right arm. In this position, he was able to hold her arms pinned against his chest, while his left hand stroked her hair and caressed her face.

"Look at me. I want you to help me with my shirt. Will you unbutton it with me?" He was looking directly into her eyes.

Joni felt her head nod yes and her traitorous fingers automatically began unbuttoning his shirt. After she had managed to get three or four buttons free, he reached down and pulled the shirt over his head and discarded it onto the floor. This process was going much too slow and he was afraid of losing her.

There he stood half naked, the most handsome man she had ever seen. Everything about him was so sensual. His thick, dark, curly hair traveled from his chest onto his stomach and lower, to a place she hadn't seen yet. Joni's hands gently stroked up and down his chest and sides exploring the feel of the hairs against her fingers. As her hands explored his stomach, they found a long and ragged scar near his left hip. When she glanced at him, he just kissed her eyes.

He wants her to know how badly he wants her physically. Both are now panting with excitement and their hearts are racing with desire. His lips began at her mouth then moved to her neck, collarbone and then they found her breasts. She sharply inhaled as he started to suckle her nipples. He can feel them become hard and elongated at the touch of his tongue.

Her head continued to nod no as she is mentally demanding her hands to push him away. But they, like every other part of her body, was yielding to his touch, ignoring the feeble orders coming from her brain.

Adam placed Joni's right hand on his pants, to feel his rock-hard erection. "Do you feel how much I want you? Joni, help me with my belt." He commanded and her hands quickly complied. Once the belt was open, Adam unfastened and unzipped his pants, dropping everything in a pile at his feet. He used the toe of one foot to push of one shoe and then the other, then stepped out of the pile of clothing.

Joni put forth no resistance. But there was still head shaking. She just continued stroking his chest and moaning at his touch. Adam was loving her body and watching how it responded. She was hot, wet and anxious to know the physical love they have been denying for so long. His tongue was exploring her body, but he realized it made her close her eyes.

He pulled this woman close to him again, then gently laid her back onto the bed while he continued kissing her neck. The length of his body was lying next to her as his mouth was exploring her body. Joni's hands found her blanket and attempted to cover herself up. Adam pulled the blanket away from her and tossed it onto the floor.

Both were breathing rapidly, anxiously anticipating. Her hands were everywhere on his body, discovering what he promised was hers, only for her. This is the danger territory, when she typically retreats to Jake's memory. Adam now must be careful to make sure that she knows what they are doing. "Oh, Joni, you are so beautiful. Look at me." Adam was up on one elbow looking into her eyes. "Keep your eyes open. I want you to see me. Say my name. Please say MY name." His voice is husky with desire as his kisses trail from her earlobe to throat.

"Adam, oh Adam." Joni kept her eyes on him as he glanced back up from suckling her breasts. He wanted to be sure her eyes were open as they moved closer to satisfying their desire. Her hands clawed at his back as he planted kisses and ran his tongue down her stomach.

With the ease of a cat, he sat up and moved between her legs. Joni tensed with this movement and brought her knees together. Now, he was just sitting there, looking at her, making sure her eyes were open, requesting, "Say my name."

Joni murmured, "Adam, Adam." as he began stroking the inside of her clamped thighs. Her hips buck up from the bed to meet his touch on her thighs. She is tense and eager to have more. When Adam feels her beginning to shudder, he stops. He knows she is close, and he must careful not to bring her too far. Adam leaned forward and planted his hands next to her shoulders. He was now on all fours, with his knees between her legs. He began kissing her face, nibbling on her lower lip, then trailing butterfly kisses to her neck.

Joni is angry at her body because it continues to betray her, lifting off the bed to greet his kisses. The desire for his touch was so intense, it seemed like her body would burst into flames. Her body continued to respond to his desire for more. Her hands were rubbing up and down his arms. One by one, he captured those hand in his and held them at her shoulders. He leaned forward and whispered, "I want you to open your legs for me. Look at me and say my name, please, Joni, keep looking at me."

Just like he asked, her knees fell further apart. Her legs parted and her knees drop toward the bed.

Now he is so hard and anxious to be inside her! His full erection slips inside her with ease, going deep. "Oh honey!"

He stills, giving her a few seconds to feel all of him. As he begins to move, her hips rise to greet every thrust. Unconsciously, she finds her back arching as he enters her. When he saw her eyes were closed he again asked her to open them.

"Say my name and open your eyes. Joni please. Say my name." He pleads softly.

"Adam. Adam, oh Adam…" She murmurs with wide open eyes. He relaxes knowing she truly knows it is him. Jake has not invaded their lovemaking.

As he began to find a rhythm, she calls his name over and over. Her hips lifted off the bed to ease all of him back inside. She matches his every movement. The tension was building with each thrust, then suddenly, everything ignited. Her body was shaking with spasms at the same time Adam released her hands so she could pull him close to her body. He collapsed the full weight of his body onto Joni. They laid there trying to catch their breath, letting their hearts relax from the stress they had just put them through.

Adam lifted his head off her chest and nibbled on her lips. He gently rolled off, reached down to the floor and brought up the blanket she had been seeking earlier. Gently he covered them both up as he snuggled next to her. His head was propped on his arm, as his other hand pushed a piece of hair out of her face, then he leaned down to kiss her again and said, "I love you, Joni, totally and completely."

Hearing those words made Joni's eyes fill with tears. When Adam saw a tear sliding down her cheek, he pushed it away and asked tenderly, "Did I hurt you?"

Joni's head was shaking no again, but the tears were becoming more frequent. She turns away from him and murmured "I told you I wasn't ready."

"Honey, you were very ready. I could feel how wet you were and how your body was responding. I know that you wanted me as much as I wanted you too. You know you love me too." He said stroking her cheek. She realized he was almost begging to hear those words in return.

"No. I can't. I told you I wasn't ready." The words came out like a slap in the face. "You don't get to decide when I love you. I decide. I told you I wasn't ready."

There goes that head nod of hers. Shit! Adam pushed himself up on one arm. His heart shocked by this declaration. "Are you kidding me? Are you trying to say you don't love me? That we didn't just make love. Wasn't that you in this bed with me? Your body reacted the same way mine did. Every iota of your being was panting to get me inside of you." He was running his fingers through his hair, hoping to find some magic words. His voice was a mixture of fear and confusion.

"I know you are afraid honey, but you survived that accident. Maybe you are afraid to feel alive again! But from everything you told me about your husband and your son, they would want you to be happy. They would want you to find love again. They would not be happy about the way you have been living or existing, I might say." he said completely bewildered by the turn of the conversation, trying to understand.

"I tried to tell you I wasn't ready. You kept pushing me and touching me. Of course, my body responded, I'm human. Plus, I would do anything to make you happy, Adam, anything." Joni cried out to him.

"Well then, Ms. Crawford, you are a liar. Because today I learned you will indeed open your legs for a good fuck. Well, you should consider yourself thoroughly fucked. Maybe with that word you can find some pleasure in what we did." He said harshly as he pushed himself into a sitting position next to her.

His verbal response inflamed her pride and her physical response was immediate. Joni's hand connected with his cheek, hard.

He could have stopped it, but he deserved her anger. Adam felt livid and knew he did not mean any of it. He just trying to hurt her because she has hurt him. The slap had caused the palm of her hand as much pain as it hurt his face and his pride.

He rubbed his cheek as he thought briefly about what he said. "You're right. I am sorry. I deserved that; because that is not how I feel about what we just did. I don't understand why it is so hard for you to say you have fallen in love with me? Your body knows you love me, hell your mind knows you love me. Why won't you let your heart love me too?" He paused, thinking what he needed to say next. This time it was his head shaking no.

21.

"Joni, I still love you and I think I always will. But I am making you this promise right now. I will never, ever lay a hand on you again. Not until I'm invited. When you can say that you love me." Adam was now standing at the side of the bed. His hand was still rubbing his cheek where she had slapped him.

Tears were slowly rolling down her cheeks and her head continued to bob back and forth as to say no. But everything he said was correct. Every bit of her loved him, even the hand that slapped him. But she could not get both her brain and heart to fall in line. When Joni looked up from her own thoughts, Adam was dressed. He was sitting at the foot of the bed, putting on his shoes. He looked at her with wet eyes and said, "I love only you, Joni. There has never been anyone else for me."

"Please don't leave me Adam, I don't want to lose you. I just need more time." She was kneeling in front of him looking into his eyes, pleading for some understanding "More time to do what exactly? I have tried everything I know to get you to love me. But YOU have to give your heart to me. I'm willing to try a bit longer, to see what happens. But from this day forward, I will come and see you, but I will not stay the night or put my hands on your body again. I really have to go. Right now, I need some air and to put some space between us." With that said, he got up and left the room without looking back.

Then Joni heard it…the door slam as he made his escape from the house.

The sound of his truck squealing away could be heard by everyone in the neighborhood. That sound opened the floodgate of tears as her body was instantly agonized with sobs.

Now tears were escaping Adam's eyes too. He sat briefly in the truck before he sped away. Before she could catch him in a moment of weakness. He had been so certain of their love for each other. How could he have been so wrong, kept running through his mind.

Joni was distraught as well. Her tears kept falling, but she reminded herself she had gotten exactly what she asked for, him out of her life. No complications of a relationship. So why the heck was she crying now. She remembered she didn't think she could handle the stress of a relationship, so her wish had been granted.

Where the rest of that day went, both were unaware. They each spent their day in torment, wondering why and how they had let a blossoming relationship slip away. Neither picked up the phone to call the other. Neither sure of what was going to happen next. And neither could imagine a life without the other.

Adam did not sleep a wink the entire night, because the questions about yesterday would not cease. Although he finally got out of the bed and went to work, absolutely nothing was accomplished for his presence in the office. All calls went straight to voicemail and no effort was made to get up from his desk for any reason. Finally, at 2 p.m., even Adam recognized what an incredible waste of time it was to be at the office. He decided to go to the gym, mostly to do something other than think.

Joni also struggled to get through the night. She dreamed of Jake and Jack when sleep finally released her from her thoughts. They were at a playground. She could hear a young Jack laughing and calling, 'push me higher daddy.' She watched and could see they were happy together…without her. The look on their faces was sheer happiness. Joni heard Jake said, 'mommy is trying to be happy too. She just needs to remember.'

Needless to say, the dream triggered emotions that were all over the spectrum. Is God letting her know they are together and doing well? Is she just a loony tune, barely holding on to reality? Now there is no Adam to keep her grounded and sane, would she completely go off the deep end and lose touch with reality completely? What is she missing that she should remember, she pondered through her tears?

In the morning, she received a text from Adam. He strongly suggested that she go to work, so as not to spend too much time alone. He also wrote that he would take care of dinner tonight. Of course, he was right. She thought how well he knows her. She will indeed drive herself mad if she keeps replaying the last two days over and over in her mind. The problem is not knowing why...why she couldn't say the words...tell him how she truly feels about him. Fortunately, he is keeping his word.

He is coming home...no, he's coming over.

The time spent at work kept her mind occupied, preventing the failed relationship from completely owning her thoughts. She busied herself by shelving and inventorying some new books. Joni felt guilty about her recent behavior, so much so that she worked fast and furiously to get the library back in order.

Adam was trying to decide how the evening would play out. He had promised to see her and it was a pledge he would keep. But, there is no way he could bear to be with her in the kitchen, bumping and touching, reaching over each other, being so completely in sync, or so he had previously thought. The safe decision was to pick up takeout food on the way over.

Joni had put her car in the garage and was coming through the back door when Adam pulled up in front of the house. He carried Chinese food containers in both hands. She swiftly trotted to the front door to hold it open for him.

He catches the surprised look when she sees the containers of food.

He smiled that breathtakingly warm smile at her and politely thanked her for her assistance. But he stepped around her, making no attempt to kiss her or look at her face. Joni noticed that under his eyes looked dark, indicating he did not sleep well last night either.

Tonight, he is in his jeans, boots and a white polo shirt. Either he had time to go home after work or he did not work today she contended. Joni is so unsure of where she stands with him that she is afraid to talk. If he says he didn't sleep, all the events of yesterday are back in the forefront of their minds, which is where they probably are anyway.

While he placed the food on the table, she grabbed plates, napkins, and eating utensils. Joni told him it smells wonderful, but he only shook his head yes in agreement.

They take their seats at the table, like all the many nights before. But on this night, they can't or don't talk to each other. Only this time the silence was not comfortable.

Adam admits to himself that she is trying hard to put them back on track, but he wants nothing more than to hold her. Actually, he wants to bed her again. To convince her that he is right about them as a couple. But he is afraid of her now.

The meal is over and the TV is on, which is the usual routine, but neither is watching, lost in their own thoughts, and neither have any idea what is playing. Adam sat in the chair, rather than on the couch with her, but he at least he stayed for the entire broadcast. He shakes his head no when she asks about cards. He just needs to be away from her and the intense desire to make love to her again.

He is certain that is what it will take for her to realize they are in a committed relationship. Joni stood in front of him and reached out to touch him, but he stopped her hand.

Adam had to block her hand to keep it from making contact, but then turned it over and kissed it softly, wanting to kiss so much more than just her hand. His heart was aching and his mind confused by her actions. When Joni looked at his face for comfort, all she could see were cold, sad eyes looking back at her. He quickly made his escape.

Her heart sank deeper into despair. How will she make him understand when he doesn't want to be here? Don't they have to be at the same emotional place for this…to work? Why doesn't he understand? Then the tirade of why doesn't SHE understand began in her mind.

This is the second night without Adam as a fixture in her life. Everything about him is rolling around her head. His smile, the cologne he wears, how he strokes her cheek, the way he puts his arm around her waist when they sleep together, the kisses, and his physical presence in her day to day life.

For Adam, day two begins without Joni. Maybe everyone was right. It should end, because he has become worthless at both jobs. If Vinnie gives him any shit today, he might just kill him. Adam is so sick and tired of ... what?

Adam dozed for a brief time when he kicked back in his desk chair. Joni is right there with him and he can smell her perfume. She flashes her smile and needs him to touch her. Her baby died. She is lonely and scared of being hurt. Only he can help her, because he the one that was there for her in the beginning and now. Startled from the reality, Adam wakes with a start.

Tonight, he will try harder he resolved. Maybe she really does only need more time. He wants her committed physically and emotionally. Otherwise, what is the point of walking away from everything? There must be a 'Joni' in his life for the sacrifice to be worth anything.

Adam appears for dinner again. They cooked chicken breasts and corn on the cob on the grill. It felt wonderful to be side by side as they prepared the food. This night almost feels normal. Cooking on the grill, looking at the yard and the garden. Adam worked to provide conversation, even though all he said was that his day had been uneventful so far. Joni told him about a couple of new books that had arrived, but were in such demand they were already checked out.

Adam struggled with control as he felt the warmth of her body when she was close. The smell of her perfume seemed to be everywhere. That smile is just for him, but as what, as a friend he wondered? All his thoughts were focused on two days ago when she was stroking him, calling out his name and responding....

Both were thinking, at least there was some civil conversation, as trivial as it was. Hopefully it was a place to start over. Tonight though, he did not stay for the news, but he did peck Joni on the check before he left.

Day three without Joni begins with Vinnie calling an evening meeting with his entire staff, which means Adam too. They are going to Luigi's in Virginia Beach. They serve some of the best authentic Italian food on the east coast. That is if you have an appetite to eat. Adam feels terrible about texting her to say he had a late meeting and cannot make it for dinner.

But her mind raced back to Claire and their embrace at the airport. Joni texted she would be happy to keep a plate warm for him or would scramble some eggs for him if he wanted something light since it sounds like they would be eating late.

His short response was 'see you around 8.' If they were at a better place, Adam knew he wouldn't miss seeing her for the world. But this is just a promise he will keep, nothing more.

Joni was folding the laundry at the kitchen table when Adam arrived. He stopped to pet Bandit before coming into the kitchen. In reality, Adam wants to be with her, at this house, where his real life happened. Laundry, gardening, cooking, walking a dog and loving. Life so real, it made him question again how it could not real for her.

As she opened the oven to get his plate for him, he said, "I'm not staying tonight. I promised I would come by, so I am here to check on you."

As he spoke he was making his way back out the front door. Joni saw he was looking haggard and exhausted. She so much wanted to run her fingers through his hair and touch his cheek, but she is afraid to after his warning. Remembering her decision to fight for this relationship, Joni spoke up. "Adam, I know you are mad at me. But if you are leaving me, then please, just don't come back. Letting go a little at a time hurts too much."

He spun around to face her. "Really, you can say that of me! I'm not letting go of us. I promised you I would try, but my feelings for you are not just friendly. I want you, I need you. The memory of us together, well, I'm having a tough time keeping my promise to keep my hands off you when we are together. It's just better for me to leave, so I don't make that mistake twice." He said as he glared at her face.

She squared herself in front of him and faced off for battle. "How do I move forward with you, for us, if you aren't here? I want us to work. I am trying to figure out why this is so hard for me. Can't you see that I am trying?" she begged him.

He was standing toe to toe with her. "Well, this is not just about your feelings, Ms. Crawford. Mine count and they are hurt. Maybe you will never come around. Maybe you are leaving me and I need to be prepared for that." he snapped back as he turned to leave. The sound of the door clanging shut rang like a gong in her mind.

Joni clutched her chest as her heart felt like it was breaking in two. Her legs became weak and she slowly sank to the floor. Her hands covered her face as the tears fell. Her body had taken his exit like a blow to her stomach. She was having a difficult time catching her breath.

As he was getting into his truck, he made the mistake of looking at her through the kitchen window. She had covered her face with her hands and sank to the floor. His heart clenched when he witnessed her collapse. Just like he helped at her accident, he instinctively knows she needs him the exact same way. He knew he could not leave her like this, in this state. She has no one to console her and she is completely alone again. This is her greatest fear realized.

When he came back into the house he just sat by her on the floor and opened his arms. When she looked at him, she saw he was offering to hold her, Joni slid across the floor and between his legs. She wrapped her arms around him as though he might push her away.

Adam initially planned only to let her hold him, but his heart is in charge tonight. Instead, he pulled her close, eliminating all space between their bodies.

The thought 'He does still love me and he wants to be here,' swirled through her mind. Now tears of joy were falling. Unfortunately, he had no way of knowing they were different. She was afraid to loosen her hold on him, to look him in the face to explain. She didn't want him to leave, ever.

He can feel her heart racing and his is matching the pace. His arms pulled her closer. The tenderness of the kisses he planted on top of her head made her sob more. Adam couldn't help himself, regardless of his promise not to touch her, he held her until the tears subsided. He knew it was his actions that had saved her once, but this time it will be his love that will save her.

Once she had calmed, Adam helped her to bed and covered her up. He promised to see her tomorrow. Remembering what had transpired on this very bed three days ago, there is no way he can be on that bed and forgive himself for bringing this trauma about. She has always been honest, admitting that she was afraid. Afraid of losing and hurting again. She thought she had lost him and her heart was broken. Adam believed she will recognize the pain of their almost lost relationship, as love, and she will see it soon.

Joni prayed for God's help to understand her heart. Her prayer was for the message to be crystal clear and no interpretation needed. Again, tonight Joni dreams are invaded by Jake. She could see him in his uniform, young and smiling. He held her hand tightly, but then she felt him let go of it. Jake looked at her, but then turned and walked away. Where Jake had stood before her, now stood a skeleton. It had to be Jake; his uniform was draped over the bones that stood before her. He was gone…again.

Joni woke from her slumber startled and weeping. The pressure in her chest was intense. Jake was always her safe place to retreat. It wasn't his death that she was grieving, but that he too had let go of her in the dream.

The tears fell again when she remembered Adam had let go of her in life. He had been kind and tried to her ease her pain last night.

Was this the crystal-clear message she prayed for earlier? She was going to be left behind again. Would she really be forced to muddle through life and again find some sibilance of peace again now that both men had left her? If both men exiting her life and living alone was meant to be her future, then what the hell did God think she was made of, was her final tearful thought before falling asleep.